Forerunner Foray

Forerunner Foray

Andre Norton

THE VIKING PRESS NEW YORK

With gratitude to Mrs. Phyllis Schlemmer, who so helpfully consented to use her talent to "read" for me, and to Mrs. Iris Comfort, who made our meeting possible

PREFACE

Parapsychology is now a subject for serious study around the world, storming barriers of long standing based on ignorance and fear. At one time it was dismissed as wild fantasy, except by those who had direct evidence to the contrary. Now it is the source of varied experiments.

Psychometry—a reading of the past history of an object by a sensitive who is sometimes not even aware of its nature—is a very old and well-documented talent. Recently the British archaeologist T. C. Lethbridge experimented in using this gift in his researches into sites and artifacts of Pict and pre-Roman Britain; one may read about the astonishing results in such books as *E.S.P., Ghost and Divining Rod,* and others.

Before beginning this book and while engaged in work upon it, I was witness to four "readings" by a sensitive who is well versed in this paranormal talent. In all four cases I supplied the object to be "read"; the results were amazing. In three cases the information delivered was clear, detailed, and related without hesitation; the fourth was more obscure since the object in question (a piece of antique jewelry) had passed through many hands.

One of the readings I could verify at once with knowledge I already possessed. Another reading, very detailed (in this instance the object was a rare and very old piece of Chinese manufacture), was verified by an expert some weeks after the reading, the true history being unknown to me before that time.

That this talent can be used in archaeology Mr. Lethbridge proved. That it may become a part of regular historical research in the future seems a good possibility.

1

Ziantha stood before the door smoothing a tight-fitting glove with her other hand. Under its clinging material her flesh tingled from the energy controls which had been woven so skillfully into that covering. She had seen the glove used, had practiced—but before this moment had never tried it to its full potential.

For a last time she mind-searched up and down the corridor. All clear, just as Ennia had promised, not that any Guildsperson ever depended on anything save his or her own wits, skills, and defenses. With that prickling hot on her palm, she reached forward and set her hand flat against the personalock. Yasa had paid a fabulous price for the loan of that glove; now it would be demonstrated whether that fee was justified.

Tongue tip pushing a little between set teeth, Ziantha waited for seconds frozen in time. Just when she was sure Yasa had lost her gamble, the door slid noiselessly into the wall. So far, so good!

Mind-seek again, to make sure there were no inner guards except those she had been trained to locate and disarm. It would seem that High Lord Jucundus was old-fashioned enough to use only the conventional protectives which were as child's toys to the Thieves' Guild. But still Ziantha made very sure, her bare hand on that girdle (wherein the supposed decorative gems were tiny but very effective detects) before she crossed into the room beyond, snapping down at that moment her dark sight band—which also masqueraded as part of an elaborate, high-fashion headdress, just as the cloak about her, at the pressure of a collar stud, was now a sight distort. The equipment she wore would have cost the yearly revenue of a small planet had it ever come to buying and selling; her own mathematical sense was not enough even to set a sum to its value.

The chamber had every luxury that could be offered on Korwar, the pleasure world. Treasures . . . but she was here for only one thing. Pulling the cloak tightly about her so that it might not brush against any piece of furniture and so discharge energy, traces of which could later be detected, Ziantha threaded a careful path to the far wall. If all went as Yasa wished, if it were a clean foray, Jucundus would never have a clue that his secrets had been penetrated. That is, until their substance had been safely sold.

With the nightsight at her service she might be in a well-lighted room. And not only was her sight an aid. Twice she paused at warnings offered by her belt detects and was able to mind-hold protection devices long enough to slip by, though each check heightened her uneasiness, drew upon her psychic energy.

On the wall was a tri-dee mural portraying an off-world scene. But she had been briefed as to the next step. With her tongue, answered by a blazing shock, she touched the latch of the glove, not daring to lift her other fingers from the detects. The glove responded by splitting down the back so she could hook it to her belt and pull her hand free.

Then the girl drew from beneath her cloak a pendant, raised it to one of the flashing stars on the wall display, pressed it there. An answering sound her ears could barely catch followed; the vibration of it was a pain in her head.

A portion of the wall lifted to display a cupboard. So far the skills and devices of the Guild had been successful. But the rest of her mission depended upon her own talents.

The cupboard safe was filled with neat piles of cubes so small she could have cradled three or four at a time in her palm. There were so many, and in a very limited time she must sort out the few that mattered, psychometrize their contents.

Her breath quickened as she set finger tip to the first in the top row. Not that, nor that— Her finger flickered on down, none in that row was what she wanted, though she guessed all had value. Jucundus's records: if all the rumors about him were true, it did not matter in the least that he had been forced into exile, his planetary holdings confiscated. With these microrecords he could still use men, build again, perhaps even to greater power.

Here! From the middle shelf she brought out the cube, pushing it above the band of her nightsight so it rested against the bare flesh of her forehead. This was the most dangerous part of her foray, for at this moment she must forget everything else—the detects on her belt, her own mind-barrier —and concentrate only on what she could "read" from the cube. Also, it had little meaning for her: no vivid pictures, only code symbols to be memorized. That was it. With a release of breath that was close to a sigh of relief, she put it back, sliding her finger along the rows seeking another. Yasa had thought two—but make very sure.

The second! Once more she had to wait out in danger that transfer of knowledge that left her so defenseless while it was in progress. Now she must make sure there was not a third cube. But her questing finger did not find one. She closed the panel, new relief flooding in. She had only to leave, to relock the door.

Once more drawing her distort cloak tight, Ziantha turned. Touch nothing else, leave no trace to be picked up. This was—

Ziantha froze. She had reached with her now ungloved hand to draw in a corner of the cloak which had threatened

3

to sweep across a small curio table. Now the edge of material fell from between her fingers, her hand stretched out farther, not by conscious will on her part, but as if her wrist had been seized in a powerful grip and jerked forward.

For a second or two the girl believed that she might have been caught in some new protect device that her belt had not been able to pick up. Then she realized that this was a psychic demand for her attention.

Never before had she had such an experience. When she psychometrized it was always by will, by her own volition. This was a demand she did not understand, which brought with it fear and the beginning of panic. On the table lay something that was "charged," just as the Guild devices were charged, with psychic energy so great it could command her attention.

Ziantha's first stab of fear faded. This was new, so the experience caught her even though she knew the danger of lingering. She had to see what demanded recognition from her by provoking such an answering surge of her talent.

Six objects on the table. There was a weird animal form carved from a semiprecious stone. A flat block of veriform rose-crystal with a gauze-winged free-flower from Virgal III imprisoned in it. A box of Styrian stone-wood and next to that one of those inter-ring puzzles made by the natives of Lysander. A trinket basket of tri-fold filigree sapphire held some acid-sweets. But the last— A lump of dusty clay, or so it looked.

Ziantha leaned closer. The lump had odd markings on it— pulling her— She snatched back her hand as if her fingers had neared leaping flames. But she had not touched that ugly lump, and she must not! She knew that if she did she would be totally lost.

Feverishly she wrapped her hand in a fold of her cloak, edged around the table as if it were a trap. For at that moment that was exactly what she felt it to be. A subtle trap,

4

perhaps set not by Jucundus but by some other power to imperil any one with her talent.

Ziantha scuttled across the room as if she were fleeing the clang of an alarm that would bring the whole city patrol. Outside in the corridor, the room again sealed, she stood breathing with the painful, rib-raising force of one who has fled for her life, fighting back the need to return, to take into her hand that lump of baked clay, or earth-encrusted stone, or whatever it was—to *know!*

With shaking hands she made those swift alterations to her clothing which concealed the double purpose of her garments, allowing her to appear a person who had every right to walk here. What was the matter with her? She had succeeded, could return to Yasa now with exactly the information she had been sent to get. Still she had no feeling of exultation, only the nagging doubt that she had left behind something of infinitely greater value, disastrously spurned.

The branch corridor united with the main one, and Rhin stepped from the shadows where he had concealed himself so well that he startled even Ziantha on his appearance. He wore the weapon belt of a personal guard, the one branch of the Thieves' Guild that had quasi-legality, since they offered protection against assassins. And some of the galactic elite who made Korwar their playground had good reason to fear sudden death.

At his glance she nodded, but they did not speak as he fell into step a pace or so behind her, as was determined by their present roles. Now and then as she moved, but not with undue haste, Ziantha caught sight of them both in a mirror. It gave her a slight shock to see herself in the trappings of a Zhol Maiden, her natural complexion and features concealed by the paint of an entertainer. Her cloak, its distort switched off, was a golden orange, in keeping with the richness of the gems in her headdress, girdle, and necklace. Garnished like

5

this, she had the haughty look that was part of her role, quite unlike her usual self.

They were on the down ramp now and here were others, a motley of clothing, of racial types, of species. Korwar was both a playground and a crossroads for this part of the galaxy. As such, its transient population was most varied. And among them her present guise attracted no attention. The company of a Zhol Maiden for an evening, a week, a month, was a symbol of prestige for many galactic lords. She had had excellent coaching from Ennia, whose semblance she wore tonight—Ennia, who companied with High Lord Jucundus, keeping him well occupied elsewhere.

They reached the main hall, where the flow of guests moving in and out, seeking banqueting halls, gaming rooms, was a steady river into which they dropped. Yet Ziantha did not turn her head even to look at Rhin, though she longed to search faces, probe. Had her venture of the evening, the drain on her talents, brought this queer feeling of being shadowed? Or was it that her meeting with that lump had shaken her into this uneasiness? She sensed—what? The pull of the rock, yes, but that was something she could and would control.

This was something different, a feeling of being watched—a Patrol sensitive? In these garments she was protected by every device the Guild possessed against mind-touch. And all knew that the Guild had techniques that never appeared on the market or were known to the authorities.

Yet she could not throw off the sensation that somewhere there was a questing—a searching. Though as yet she was sure it had not found her. If it had she would have known instantly.

Rhin went ahead, summoned a private flitter with a Zhol registration. Ziantha pulled up the collar of her cloak as she went into the night, sure now that her imagination was overactive, that she need not fear anything at all—not now.

Tikil was all jewels of light, strains of music, exuberant life,

6

and she felt the lifting of a burden, began to enjoy the knowledge that she had repaid tonight the long years of training and guardianship. Sometimes lately she had chafed under that indebtedness, though Yasa had never reminded her of it. Still Ziantha was not free—would she ever be?

But at least she was freer than some. As their flitter climbed to the upper lanes, swung out in a circle to bring them to Yasa's villa, they crossed the edge of the Dipple, where the jeweled lights of the city were cut off by that wedge of gloom as dark and gray as the huddle of barracks below were by day, as depressing to the spirit to see as they were to those who still endured a dreary existence within their drab walls.

Almost her full lifetime the Dipple had been there, a blot that Korwar, and this part of the galaxy, tried to forget but that could not destroy.

Ziantha need only look down on that grayness as they swept over to realize that there were degrees of freedom and that what she now had was infinitely preferable to what lay down there. She was one of the lucky ones. How could she ever doubt that?

All because Yasa had seen her on begging detail that time at the spaceport and had witnessed the guessing trick she had taught herself. She had thought it was only a trick, something anyone could do if he wished. But Yasa had known that only a latent sensitive could have done as well as Ziantha. Perhaps that was because Yasa was an alien, a Salarika.

Through Yasa's interest she had been brought out of the Dipple, taken to the villa, which had seemed a miracle of beauty, put to school. Though the Salarika had demanded instant obedience and grueling hours of learning, it was all meat and drink to Ziantha, who had starved and thirsted for such without knowing it before. She was what those months and years of training had made her, an efficient tool of the Guild, a prized possession of Yasa's.

Like all her feline-evolved race, Yasa was highly practical, utterly self-centered, but able to company with other species to a workable degree without ever losing her individuality. Her intelligence was of a very high order, even if she approached matters from a slightly different angle than would one of Ziantha's species. She had great presence and powers of command and was one of the few fems who had risen to the inner ranks of the Guild. Her own past history was a mystery; even her age was unknown. But on more than one planet her slightly hissed word was law to more beings than the conventional and legal rulers could control.

Ziantha was a human of Terran—or past-Terran—descent. But from what race or planet she had come in that dim beginning, when the inhabitants of dozens of worlds (the noncombatants, that is) had been driven by war to land in the "temporary" camp of the Dipple, she could not tell. Her appearance was not in any way remarkable. She had no outstanding features, hue of skin, inches of height, which could easily place her. And because she was unremarkable in her own person, she was of even more value. She could be taught to take on the appearance of many races, even of one or two nonhuman species, when there was need. Like Yasa, her age was an unsolved question. It was apparent she was longer in maturing than some races, though her mind absorbed quickly all the teaching it was given, and her psychic talent tested very high indeed.

Gratitude, and later the Guild oath, bound her to Yasa. She was part of an organization that operated across the galaxy in a loose confederacy of shadows and underworlds. Governments might rise and fall, but the Guild remained, sometimes powerful enough to juggle the governments themselves, sometimes driven undercover to build in the dark. They had their ambassadors, their veeps, and their own laws, which to defy was quick death. Now and then the law itself dealt with the Guild, as was true in the case of Jucundus.

The Dipple was well behind now as they cruised above the gardens and carefully preserved bits of wild which separated villa from villa. Ziantha's hands clenched under the border of her cloak. The thought of tonight's work—not the work, no, rather that lump—filled her mind. An ache as strong as hunger gripped her.

She must see Ogan as soon as she discharged into the waiting tapes the memories she carried—she must see Ogan, discover what was the matter. This obsession which rode her was not natural, certainly. And it upset her thinking, could be a threat to her talent. Ogan, the renegade parapsychologist who had trained her, was the only one who could tell her the meaning of this need.

The flitter set down on a landing roof, where a dim light was sentinel. As a cover Yasa claimed a Salariki headhood of a trading firm and so possessed a profitable and legal business in Tikil. That establishment she ran with the same efficiency as she did her Guild concerns. Nor was she the only one within that organization to live a double existence. On Korwar she was the Lady Yasa, and her wealth brought respect and authority.

Ziantha sped across to the grav shaft. Late as it was, the house was alive, as usual, though the sounds were few and muted. But there was never any unawareness under a roof where Yasa ruled. As if only by eternal vigilance could she continue to hold in her long clawed hands the threads of power she must weave together for her purposes.

At the scratch of her fingernails on a plexiglass panel into which had been set a glory of ferns, that panel rolled back, and Ziantha faced the heavily scented chamber of Yasa's main quarters. On the threshold she paused dutifully while blowers of perfumed spray set up about that portal gave her a quick bath of the scent which was Yasa's preference at the moment.

Quite used to this, Ziantha allowed her cloak to slip to the floor, turned slowly amid the puffing of vapor. To her own sense of smell the odor was oppressively powerful; to the Salarika it made her acceptable as a close companion. It was the one weakness of the species, their extreme susceptibility to alien scents. And they took precautions to render their lives among aliens bearable in this way.

As she endured that anointing, Ziantha lifted off the headdress of Zhol fashion. Her head ached, but that was only to be expected after the strain she had put on her talent and nerves tonight. Once she had delivered what she brought, Ogan might entrance her into a healing sleep, if she asked for it.

The light in the room was subdued, again because of the mistress here. Yasa did not need bright illumination. She was curled among the cushions which formed her favorite seat. By the open window was an eazi-rest, in which Ogan lay at full length. The rumors, which were many, said that he was a Psycho-tech, one of the proscribed group. Like Yasa, he was ageless on the surface, and could well have had several life-prolonging treatments. But on what world he had been born no one knew.

Unlike the Salarikis who served in Yasa's villa, he was a small frail man, seeming a desiccated shadow beside them. He was not only a master of mental talents, but he possessed certain infighting skills which made him legend. Now he lay with his head turned away, facing the open window, as if the strong perfume bothered him. However, as Ziantha came forward, he turned to watch her, his face expressionless as always.

In that single moment the girl knew that she had no intention of telling him about the lump. Ogan might give her peace, but that she did not want at the price of letting him know what had surprised and frightened her. Let that remain her secret—at least for now. Why should Ogan be always full master?

"Welcome—" there was a purring in Yasa's voice. She was slim, and the most graceful creature in movement Ziantha had ever seen. And, in her way, the most beautiful as well. Black hair, more like plushy fur, was thick and satiny on her head and shoulders and down the upper sides of her arms. Her face, not quite as broad and flat as those of most of her species, narrowed to an almost sharply pointed chin. But it was the wonder of her very large eyes which drew away attention from all other features. Slanted a little in her skull, their pupils contracting and expanding in degrees of light, like those of her far-off feline ancestors, these were a deep red-gold, their color so vivid against her naturally grayish skin as to make them resemble those koros stones that were the marvel and great wealth of her home world.

Two such stones were set now in a wide collar about her throat, but they seemed dimmed by her eyes, even though they radiated slightly in the low-lighted room.

She put forth a hand equipped with retractable nails now sheathed in filigree metal caps, and beckoned Ziantha. Her short golden robe, caught in by a girdle from which hung scent bags, shimmered as she moved. From down in her throat came a tiny murmur of sound the girl knew of old. Yasa purred, Yasa was well pleased.

"I do not ask, cubling, if all went well. That is apparent in your presence here. Ogan—"

He did not answer her, but the eazi-rest moved, bringing him upright. It was his turn to beckon Ziantha. She sat down on a stool near the table and picked up the waiting headband. Stripping off the long, now far too hot wig, she slipped the band over her own close-cropped hair. A few minutes more and she would be free of all the knowledge she had brought with her. For following her report, the machine that recorded it would purge her memory of factors it might be dangerous for her to know. It was a safeguard her kind had demanded before they would use their talents, so that they could not be forced by any enemy to talk after such a mission.

The girl unlocked her memory, knowing that every symbol she had read from the cubes was being recorded. What if she kept on, allowed the machine to read and then erase her reaction to the lump? But if she did that, those already reading her report on the visa-screen of the machine would know it too. No—her hand moved close to the cut-off key—she would prevent that.

There. Her finger came down and she experienced the familiar moment or two of giddiness, of disorientation. Now she would remember up to the opening of Jucundus's safe and after, but not what she had "read."

"Excellent." Yasa's purr was louder when Ziantha was again aware of the room and those about her. "A first-level foray in every way. Now, cubling, you must be most tired—go to your nest."

She was tired, achingly tired. The lifting of her mental burden drained her, as it always did, though this was her first really big foray. Those in the past had been but token employment compared to this. Ogan was at her side with a cup of that milky looking restorative. She gulped that avidly and went to gather up her cloak and headdress.

"Fair dreams." Yasa's lips wrinkled in her equivalent of a smile. "Dream of what you wish most, cubling. For this night's work I shall make it yours."

Ziantha nodded, too tired to answer with words. What she wanted most—that was no idle promise. Yasa would indeed make it come true. Those of the Guild were not niggardly with anyone who brought off a successful top foray. What she wanted most now was sleep, though not of Ogan's sending.

Back in her own chamber Ziantha pulled off the rest of the Zhol dress, dropped the trappings in a bundle on the floor. Tired as she was, she would not go to bed with that stiff, cracking mask of paint and overleaf on her face. She went into the fresher, set the dials, stepped into the waves of cleansing vapor. It was good to be her real self again.

As if to assure herself she had returned to Ziantha, she looked into the cruelly bright mirror, cruel because being so often used to check a disguising makeup, it revealed rather than softened every defect of complexion and feature. There was the real outward Ziantha. And with this hour and her great fatigue, that sight was a blow to any vanity.

She was very thin and her skin was pallid. Her hair, from the warm steam of her bath, curled tightly to her head, no lock of it longer than one of her fingers. In color it was silver fair, though in daylight it would show a little darker. Her eyes were gray, so pale as to seem silver too. The mouth below was large, her lips with little curve, but a clear red. As for the rest— She scowled at the true Ziantha and shrugged on her night robe, letting the light of that revelation die behind her as she left the room.

Dream of what she wanted most, Yasa had said. What if she asked for a complete cosmetic-change—to be someone else all the time, not just at those intervals when she played games for the Guild? Would Yasa agree to that? Perhaps she would, if Ziantha asked, but she only played with the idea.

But of course, what she wanted most—right now—was that lump of clay or carved stone. To have it right here in her two hands that she might learn its secret!

Ziantha gasped. What had put that in her mind? She had not been thinking of it at all, and then—suddenly—there it was as clear as if she could indeed reach out and cup it in her palms. And she did want it. What had happened to her this night?

Shivering, she ran to the bed, threw herself into its soft hollow, and pulled the covers up over her trembling body —even over her head.

2

Ziantha awoke suddenly from a sleep where, if dreams had crowded, she could not remember, as if she had been summoned. She knew what she must do, as surely as if Yasa had given her an order. Fear chilled her small body, but greater than that fear was the need which was a hunger in her.

The girl remembered Ogan's precept: fear, faith, and obsession were akin. All three could drive a person to complete self-abandonment, removing mind blocks, unleashing emotions. She did not fear that much, but she knew she was obsessed.

Korwar's sun was above the horizon. These chambers were all soundproof; she had only her knowledge of the daily routine to guide her. The quickest way to arouse interest in Yasa's domain was to depart from the usual. Ziantha drew herself into a small brooding bundle on the window seat, laced her arms about her knees, and stared down into the garden.

It was going to be a fair day—good. Psychic powers diminish in a storm. Her talent could also be threatened by other factors; energy fields produced by machines, the sun, planets, even human emotions. What she had in mind was a stern test. She might not be able to do it at all, even if she could station herself at the right site, at the proper moment, with the needed backing.

The needed backing—

Psychokinetic power—

14

There were devices in plenty in Ogan's lab. But to lay finger on one of those was to attract instant attention. She must depend upon another source entirely.

Ziantha unclasped her hands, raised them to cover her eyes, though she had already closed them, concentrated on forming a mind-picture and with it a summons. It would depend on whether Harath was free.

She delivered her message. But so far she was favored; Harath was not in the lab. Quickly she went to the fresher, bathed, and sat down before the merciless mirror, no longer intent upon her own shortcomings, but upon applying those aids that would take her into Tikil as a person exciting no second glance.

A companion of the second class, from Ioni, she decided. The factors, such as her height, that she could not alter without wasting some of her power in producing a visual hallucination, would fit that identity. The girl worked swiftly, a wig of brassy-colored hair brushed out in full puffing, the proper skin tint, lenses slipped in, changing her own pale eyes to a much darker hue.

She chose skin-hugging trousers of a metallic blue, a side-slitted overrobe of green, and then hesitated over jewelry that was, for the most part, more than jewelry if carefully examined. Best not, she decided regretfully. Some of those devices had side effects that could be picked up by Patrol detects. Stick to a shoulder collar with no secondary use, wrist rings that covered the back of her hands with a wide, flexible mesh of worked gold between the five joined finger rings and the wrist bracelet, forming mitts without palms.

A last check in the mirror assured her the disguise was complete. She dialed the combination code for morning juice and vita meal and ate to the last crumb and drop that sustaining, if unexciting, breakfast.

Her corridor was silent, but she knew the house was astir. Now the last test— Drawing upon all the resolution and ease she could summon, Ziantha stepped to the visa-panel block and punched a code button.

She thus recorded her present appearance and gave her reason for leaving the villa. Without that her absence would arouse suspicion, although the fact that she went into Tikil in disguise was of no moment. It was customary for those of Yasa's household to make sure of cover in the city.

"I go to Master-Gemologist Kafer on the Ruby Lane," she said. Well enough. Yasa would believe that she might be selecting the promised reward for last night. A gem would be such. And Kafer's shop would place her close to her real destination.

For a moment Ziantha waited, tense. There might be a negative flash in answer. It could be her misfortune that Ogan had set up a plan of some experiment this morning. But only the white flicker of a recording came in return.

Though she wanted to run, to be out of reach of either Ogan or Yasa as quickly as she could, Ziantha disciplined herself to keep to the almost strolling pace of one embarking for a morning's shopping in Tikil. She dared not even summon Harath again, not when Ogan's devices might record such a call. But, before her tight rein on impatience was stretched too far, she was on the roof, where a flitter waited.

One of Yasa's liege-fighters turned his head, his eyes slitted against the full light of the sun striking across them. It was Snasker, a taciturn, older warrior, his pointed ears fringed with old battle scars, another of which ridged his jawline. He was holding out one hand while a shape of soft down jumped to catch at his fingers. His glance at Ziantha was indifferent.

"For Tikil?" His voice was a low growl.

"Yes. If it pleases you, Snasker."

He yawned. "It pleases, fem." Snapping two claws at his companion, he climbed into the flitter.

Ziantha stooped to catch the little creature who now threw himself into her arms, chittering a welcome. Though she could not understand his speech, she met mind-talk easily.

"Harath here. Go with Ziantha now, now!"

She beamed back agreement and settled herself beside Snasker. Harath sat on her lap, panting a little, his beaked mouth open a fraction, his round eyes wide to their fullest extent.

Just what Harath was, what species he represented, or whether he could be classed as "human" or merely as a highly evolved and telepathic animal, Ziantha did not know. His small body was covered with a down which could be either feathers or the lightest and fluffiest fur. But he was wingless, having coiled within deep pockets of his body-covering four short tentacles he could use as one might use rather clumsy arms and hands. His legs and feet were down-covered, though the down was shorter in length and fluffed out as if he were wearing leggings and three-toed slippers on his feet. The toes ended in wicked-looking talons which matched the oddly vicious warning of his large, curved beak. In color he was blue-gray; his eyes, black rimmed, were a vivid blue.

He had come to Ogan still encased in his natal egg, so transported during the incubation period, by a Guild collector. And his talent was psychokinetic to a high degree. Not that he apported as well as Ogan had hoped—perhaps that was because he was still so young, and his powers would grow. But he could "step-up" the psychic power of another to an amazing degree.

On Korwar, in Tikil, where outré pets were the rule rather than the exception, he excited little attention. He chaffed against wearing the small harness Ziantha now fitted on, enduring it only because he must. Harath had a vast curiosity, and his favorite treat was a trip away from the villa. Since Ogan had decided such trips were a form of training, it was not unusual for Harath to accompany any one of the household into town.

The sun was very brilliant and on her knees Harath's small body vibrated with the soft click-click of beak with which he expressed contentment.

"Where?" Snasker asked.

"I go to Kafer's."

They were winging over the Dipple but Ziantha would not look at that. She was excited by what she planned, deadly afraid she might betray some of that feeling to Harath. This —this must be like chewing gratz—this sensation that one could do anything if one only set one's determination to it.

She must hold control, she must! Fight down that tingle of energy which came into being at the end of one's spine, rising slowly to the head. Not here—not yet!

The flitter landed on a platform in the center of the gardened square. Through the trees she could see the flashing jewels of light which marked Ruby Lane of the gem merchants —the brilliant signal visible even in the sun. Now she must curb her impatience, visit Kafer in truth before she tried her experiment.

Normally she would have been totally distracted by Kafer's display. It was sheer pleasure to those who loved the beauty of gems cut and polished. Or else the small toys and oddments, both old and new, made of precious things gathered up from perhaps a thousand worlds to show here, where credits flowed a free river.

In spite of the need which drove her, Ziantha stood for a moment entranced before a diadem lined with small tubes set with flexible thread-thin filaments, each supporting a flower, a leaf, a bud, or a filmy insect, to form a halo which would sway like meadow grass under a breeze with every movement of the wearer. Beyond this was a town made of karem—that iridescent precious metal of a long-lost alloy from Lydis IV—complete in miniature with even its population, each tiny inhabitant no taller than her thumbnail but equipped with microscopic features and apparel.

She could look and look, but this was not what brought her here. Though most of Tikil kept late hours and the press of shoppers would not come until afternoon, there were customers drifting in and out of the shops, from Kafer's at the proud head of Ruby Lane, all down the road.

Harath rode on her shoulders as she moved along, the leash of his harness looped about her forearm; his head sometimes seemed to turn almost completely around as he tried to see everything at once. Ziantha did not mind-talk, saving energy for later. She forced herself to saunter, pausing here and there.

Now she had reached the end of the lane, and she could wait no longer. Ziantha turned to cross into the luxurious foliage of the garden, nearer to the building which held Jucundus's apartment. She must get as close to that as she could.

Unfortunately she was not the only weary shopper to seek out the shade and rest here. Each bench she came to had its occupant. And the closer she came to her goal, the more crowded these ways appeared to be. Her frustration became almost unbearable when added to the strain of keeping control. Somewhere there must be a place! She was not going to surrender her plan so easily.

Her agitation reached Harath. He was chittering unhappily, shifting his feet about on her shoulder with his claws pricking through to her skin. If she got him too upset he would not perform.

They were almost to the end of the last walk when Ziantha came upon something that might have been intended by fortune for the very purpose she had in mind—a small side way between two Stick palms. She turned into that hopefully, finding a moment later a bench sheltered by growth, almost invisible from the main path, and unoccupied.

The reason for that was plain. Dew had condensed on the

plants and wet the surface of the seat with droplets which the sun had not dried because of the heavy screen of foliage overhead. She looked at that and, with a sigh, jerked up her slitted skirt, seating herself gingerly on the damp surface, the chill of which penetrated through her single layer of clothing at once. But more than this minor discomfort was she willing to risk for her plan.

She summoned resolution, removed Harath gently from her shoulder, and turned him about on her knee to face her, feeling the flow of communication between them as his eyes locked on hers. Yes, he was willing to aid her, not needing to be coaxed.

Now Ziantha released that brake on her power she had maintained through the morning. The pulse of energy in her lower back built up slowly, perhaps inhibited by the control. But it was rising to her call, climbing up through her shoulders, now at the nape of her neck, coming at last behind her forehead, pulsing faster in a rhythm that was comforting. She felt her whole being at acute attention, as always happened when she called upon this ability, about which even Ogan knew so little.

The time was—now!

Ziantha no longer stared into Harath's eyes. Rather she fastened on the mind picture that had haunted her since last night. It was as if she no longer dwelt within her body, but rather hung suspended above that table, a swimmer in the air, anchored in place by her desire, her need for that crude lump.

Summoning every fragment of memory, the girl built her mental picture into vivid reality. Now—come! All of her talent surged to feed her desperate desire. And there was that stronger pulse of energy bolstering it, the energy Harath released. Come! As if she shouted that to something which could easily obey her cry, Ziantha shaped that demand in her mind, imprisoning the lump as if her order were a tangible net. *Come!*

She held that at peak force as long as she could. But there came a time when, even with Harath's backing, she could keep it so no longer. It swept away, leaving her so spent she swayed dizzily. Pain ran in ripples along her arms and legs as she became aware of her body again. Her hands dropped from their grasp on the alien, twitching in a lack of coordination. Saliva dribbled from her mouth, sticky wet on her chin. She had never unleashed such a will-to-do before and she was frightened at her present weakness, at the dizzy swirl of bush and tree when she looked up.

Harath chittered and pressed against her; there was fear in his nuzzling. If this had so affected her, what might it have done to him? For the first time that day, thought of another broke through the obsession which had haunted her since waking. Ziantha tried to raise her hands to soothe him, found they were numbed, deadened, moved slowly and clumsily.

But—

There was something else. In Harath's struggle to get nearer he had almost shoved it to the ground. Dazedly she brought her hand up to catch it—the lump!

She had done it! A successful apport! She did not rate high on the scale of psychokinetic power, yet with Harath's backing she had brought it here!

Only now she was so drained, so weak, she could hardly force one thought to meet another in her head. She had wanted, she had so fiercely wanted— But now that it lay there on her knee, what did she plan to do with it? She could not think, not yet. It was like trying to catch one's breath after a grueling race; the plight of her body was too intrusive; to it she must surrender for now.

Slowly, far too slowly, her strength began to return. In this side nook, shadowy as it was, Ziantha could not even be sure of the passing of time as man normally lived it. For in the realm into which she had forced herself, time had a different measurement entirely. She could have sat there for a few moments—or hours. The chill of the damp seat struck inward and she was shivering. Yet she could not summon strength enough to get to her feet, out into the heat of the sun.

And she could look at that brown-gray lump with indifference. Only, as she continued to stare at it, that indifference changed. The wild excitement that had gripped her at her first contact with it was growing again. It was worth it! She knew that it was worth any effort she had had to put forth. It was—what—? She knew only that she must find out, that such knowledge was as necessary to her as breathing or thinking—

But she dared not tap it now, not while she was so shaken by the effort made to apport it from Jucundus's apartment to this place. No, she must have the backing of all her energy when she tried to break its secret. Which meant she dared not touch it with her bare hand.

Very awkwardly, for still her hands were numb, Ziantha tugged at her girdle, forced open her sling purse, and, using a portion of her skirt wrapped around her fingers to keep from direct contact, wedged and pushed the chunk into the purse for safekeeping. It was a quite visible lump but the best she could do.

Food—drink—Ziantha had remembered seeing a small serving grotto in the other path. With Harath clinging to the bodice of her robe as she managed to stand erect, she paced slowly toward that haven, striving to fight off dizziness.

Back in the full sun the warmth seeped into her body, displacing that chill, banishing the shivers which had wrung her moments before. Harath climbed now to grip her shoulder once again. Though the energy that had flowed to her from him had been great, still it seemed that their ordeal had not affected him as it had her. That so small a body and brain could have generated that powerful backup was a surprise to her, as she, in turn, began to throw off the mind-dulling fatigue.

Ziantha came to the grotto and wavered into the nearest seat. As she sat down, the listing of drinks and food beamed up at her from the top of her table. She punched the proper buttons to bring her the most sustaining of those dishes.

Chewing on a vita-biscuit, the girl did not forget Harath. She broke off bits, dipped them into a conserve high in energy quotients, and passed them to him. The first shock had worn away; even the pains in her legs and arms were easing as she drank the thick, sweet lingrum juice, its warmth adding to the sun's to banish the last of the chill.

Now, with the ebbing of the worst of her fatigue, Ziantha began to feel a new exuberance. She had done it—had apported, a feat she had never tried before, beyond a few tests in the lab. Most of those had rated her ability too low to warrant concentrated training. Of course she had not done it alone; she could not have. But it was her thought, her plan that had accomplished it. Now the girl longed to take the lump out of her purse, to inspect it. However, good sense kept her from doing so.

Harath's long tongue snaked from his bill as he licked some drops of sweet from the fluff on his chest. Then suddenly, he froze, and through the tautness of his body an alert reached Ziantha, though he did not try to communicate with mind-talk. Slowly his head turned in one of those hardly-to-be-believed side sweeps, so that he was looking almost squarely, not only over her shoulder, but also over his own. And Ziantha nearly cried out as his talons tightened, piercing the fabric of her robe. She sat with the cup raised in both hands to her lips, but she no longer sipped at its contents.

Rather she readied her powers as best she could and sent forth a mind-seek.

Harath had his own protection, and that did not depend, save in a last extremity, upon his five senses, but rather on the sixth, or seventh, or whatever number made up his "sensitive" reaction to any threat. He was alert to something now, and the fact that he did not relay what he had picked up to her was a greater warning of danger.

Her earlier exultation was wiped away. She had spent herself too much in that burst of kinetic seeking; her mind-search was now limited, picking up nothing of moment. Ogan? Had he trailed them to Tikil? She could believe that. He might just have set up this whole affair, Ziantha thought. He could have suspected last night that she had held back something in her report, used her to uncover that today. Now it seemed, looking back, that it had all been far too easy —her leaving the villa with Harath—all of it!

She wanted desperately to turn her head, sure that if she did so she would see Ogan come into view. And there was no use running; he could mark her down in an instant by any one of four or five devices she understood only too well.

Harath stirred. He was climbing down from her shoulder, clutching at her robe with his claws, using his two upper tentacles to balance. Then he squatted on the table, flicking forth one of those tentacles, inserting it greedily into the pot of sweet spread, whipping it back to draw through his beak, his tongue curled about it to sweep off the last bit.

But he was acting. Just as she had acted out the role of Zhol Maiden last night. Now he was all small-creature-with-but-a-thought-of-food. And Ziantha, not quite sure how she understood (unless Harath could broadcast on some more subtle mental length) concentrated on watching him. Lick, eat, lick, eat. He did not turn his head again. But now and then he bobbed it energetically up and down, licking splashes of his treat from his chest.

Up—down—slow—now twice fast—Ziantha caught her breath. Harath—Harath was coding! She spread out her hand on the side of the cup as she drank, but her fingers tapped that surface with the same beat.

Bob, bob, bob—she read his warning of a sensitive. Not Ogan—Harath would have no reason to warn of him. To the alien Harath, she and Ogan were of a kind, united. No, this was a stranger. And—

He might only be cruising. One of the Patrol sensitives taping mind levels as their companions, who used physical means of controlling crime, made inspections through those districts where the activities of the Guild might be centered.

Ziantha had been proud of her achievement; now her folly struck her like a forceful blow. If there had been a sensitive anywhere within range of her late exploit, the amount of energy she had loosed would have brought instant investigation. That was why Harath was using code. As long as neither of them tried mind-search they were safe, at least from a spot check. Certainly on suspicion alone no patroller could pick up innocent wayfarers for psychic testing.

Her fingers moved on the mug. Harath bobbed his head. They understood each other. Her one fear was the distance now between them and means of escape. She felt far better than she had when she had crawled out into this place. But she would have to stroll, not hurry, to the flitter park, and she must plan a return route to baffle any trail. Could she trust her exhausted body?

Also, any Patrol sensitive might well be able to recognize the signs of energy exhaustion. He had only to note the least wavering on her part and take her in to be psyched. And then— But she would not let herself think about what would come after that. No, she must summon up all her resolution and make it to the flitter landing without displaying any overt signs to any watcher.

It was growing late, and she could not remain here too

long. This place might already have been marked down as one of the sites to look, the need for food and drink . . . Ziantha fumbled for a tal-card made out on a legal business of Yasa's, slipped it into the payment slit. Harath climbed once more to her shoulder as she stood up.

Good. She could walk without believing that each new step was going to spill her forward on her face, that much had food done for her. Now, the flitter park—slow and easy, but not too slow.

Harath had closed his eyes. For all intents he might be sleeping, though his sharp hold on her shoulder did not waver. He had closed his mind, just as she had closed hers. But as she went she used her eyes. Her companion had signaled "he" in relation to the hunter. But the pursuer might just as well be a woman. Four, five, six—a dozen people in sight.

Some were obviously visitors, or at least not in a hurry. There were three others—all men—wearing the dress of merchants. If she could have used mind-touch only for an instant she would know the enemy, but that would have revealed her in turn. Now she must mark faces, make very sure none could follow her back to the villa. All at once that seemed to her to be a very safe refuge.

3

She reached the lift to the flitter landing and was borne aloft, wishing she dared to look back and so sight a follower. But her years of training held, and she drew about her as best she could a concealing cloak of unconcern. A few moments later she dialed the call signal for a robo-flitter. Those last seconds of waiting for the empty transport to slide in before her were the worst, so close to escape, yet at any moment subject to challenge.

The flitter dropped, its cabin door opened, and Ziantha scrambled in with perhaps more haste than was cautious, already reaching for the code key to tap out a destination to confuse the trail. Also she risked a quick glance back at the platform from which she was rising. No sign of pursuit.

But that was no proof that she was not under observation.

Minutes later the flitter set down at the wide and crowded general market just beyond the fringe of the landing port. The dealers who traded here bought from space crewmen, who legally could dabble in the private commerce of small objects, and illegally in contraband. Here the Guild had many contacts planted at strategic points, and no sensitive could pierce their protects. Ziantha relaxed—as much as she could with that lump in her purse—as she threaded a way through the narrow runways between one booth and the next. From those contacts she might claim transportation back to the villa to baffle any ordinary Patrol exercise.

She had the pricking of the band on her left wrist to guide

her to the stall where she might claim aid, as that was acti-vated to pick up a Guild signal. Twilight was close, Harath clicked his beak in a warning, fluffing up his down. He did not take kindly to the rising chill of night.

A blink sign proclaimed the name of Kackig, and Ziantha turned there in obedience to her own recognition prick. The man who faced her was as gray-skinned as any Salariki, but without the feline features of that species, clearly more hu-manoid as to ancestry, in spite of color.

Ziantha raised her hand as if to settle one of the flower-headed pins in her brush of wig, displaying to the full her wrist ring.

"Gentle fem." His voice was a thin pipe, seeming not to issue from his throat but from some place outside his body. "Look you—here lie the scents of a hundred stars. Breathe Flame Spice from Andros, Diamond Dust of Alaban—"

"You have Sickle-lily of the Tenth Day Bloom?"

His expression did not change beyond that of a polite merchant's attention. "By the favor of Three-horned Math, it is ready to pour into your hand, gentle fem, rare as it is. But not here, as you well know. Such a delicate fragrance is easily tainted in the open." He clapped his hands sharply, and a small boy wearing his livery overalls arose from the ground behind the stall.

Kackig snapped his fingers. "Take the gentle fem to Laros—"

Ziantha nodded her thanks and hurried to keep up with the boy, who slipped far more easily than she among the narrow and well-crowded ways of the mart. They came at last to where the delivery flitters parked in a dusty row.

"The fourth." Her guide underlined his information by pointing with a grubby finger. He surveyed what lay about them. "Now!" She crossed the short open space to enter the flitter.

There was a Salariki at the controls who glanced around

as if to assure himself she was not an intruder. From the interior also came the subtle fragrance of the Sickle-lily, which the dried petals of the Tenth Day Bloom could retain for years. Yasa's favorite scent was about to be delivered to the villa.

For the first time since Harath's first warning, the girl dared use mind-touch with her downy companion.

"We are free?"

"Now." If thought could convey a feeling of irritation, then Harath's curt reply was shadowed by that emotion. He did not add to that, which was not usual, but Ziantha did not press. Now that she was reasonably safe, the fact that she carried with her that which she had no business to have taken began to weigh on her spirits.

It all depended upon how important the apport was. If it had no more meaning for Jucundus than any other of the exotic curiosities which had been with it, then it might not even be missed for some time. And, surely if it did have importance, it would not have been left lying in full sight on the table. It would have been sealed in the safe.

She rested her hand over the bulge in her purse, haunted by the same ambivalence of desires that had ridden her ever since this spell had fallen on her. She wanted to use the lump as a focus for exploration, yet she feared it. But she believed now that her desire for knowledge was greater than her fear. It must be, or it would not have pushed her to risk so much in order to get the lump into her possession.

That she intended to keep it a secret—yes. Not that she could for long, because of Harath. He would share information with Ogan. And to suggest that he not do so would be to make sure that he would. One could not credit Harath with human motives. He was programmed to work by an alien set of impulses—which meant—

Harath snapped his beak peevishly, avoiding mind-touch. She set him on the ground as she left the flitter at the villa in-park, and he disappeared with a flash of speed surprising for his small body. Ziantha took warning from that flight and hurried to her own room. If she were to have any use at all from what she had found, it must be here and now.

Dropping among her cushions, she took out the lump, this time without precautions against touching it. Cupping it in her hands she brought it to her forehead, as if at any moment Ogan and Yasa might break in to wrest it away from her.

She swayed, almost crumpled. That thrust of instant reply was as strong as a harsh blow in the face. And yet—she could sort nothing out of the whirl of impressions that rushed so upon her. The worst was a freezing fear, the like of which she had never known before in her life. Perhaps she screamed as it closed about her; she did not know.

But that overpowering force was gone. Ziantha crouched, staring stupidly at her hands, which lay limply on her knees. The lump—the *thing*—where was it? She shrank from it when she saw it among the cushions as she might from a sudden attack by an alien creature.

Nor could she bring herself to touch it again, though that fear had ebbed, and once more she could feel the faint stirrings of the obsession which had made her covet it. Ziantha dragged herself up, tottered into the fresher, needing to feel the cleansing of water, heat, life, the knowledge that she was herself—Ziantha and not—

"Not who?" She cried that aloud this time, her hands to her head. As she ran she shed wig, clothing, to stand in as hot a mist vapor as her body could tolerate. The warmth that enfolded her skin slowly penetrated to reach that part of her which seemed to remain frozen.

Wrapped in a loose robe, she reluctantly returned to her room. Could she bundle the lump up in a covering—perhaps then bury it in the garden? Still she was drawn to it against her will, though at least she could control herself to the point of not touching it.

Ziantha went on her knees by the cushions, studying the artifact with attention she had not given it when she made that first impulsive attempt to unriddle its secret. Though its appearance was very rough, it was, she was sure, not merely some unworked lump of hard-backed clay or stone. It bore the rude semblance of a crouching figure, so rude one could not rightly say that it was meant to resemble either a monster or a man. There appeared to be four limbs of sorts attached to a barrel body. But the head, if it had even been given one, had vanished. Somehow she believed it had been conceived as it now was.

That it was old past her judging she knew. This extreme age could well have caused that nauseating whirl of impressions from her "reading," for the longer any object wrought by intelligence was in existence, the more impressions it could pick up and store, letting those forth as a chaotic mingling of pictures. It would require many sessions, much careful researching, to untangle even a small fraction of what might be packed into this grotesque object.

For a long time it had been a proved fact that any object wrought by intelligence (or even a natural stone or similar object that had been used for a definite purpose by intelligence) could record. From the fumbling beginnings of untrained sensitives, who had largely developed their own powers, much had been learned. It had been "magic" then; yet the talent was too "wild," because all men did not share it, and because it could not be controlled or used at will but came and went for reasons unknown to the possessors. So that at one instance there had been amazing and clear results that could not be questioned by witnesses, and on a second try, nothing at all.

There had been frauds when those who had reputations of wonder workers could not produce the results called for, and in desperation had turned to trickery. But always there had been a percentage that was unexplained. When man learned to study instead of to scoff, when the talented ones were neither scorned nor feared, progress began. Mind-touch was as well accepted as speech now, and with it all those other "unexplainables" which had been denied for generations. Then when mankind of Ziantha's own species—that first mankind which had neither mutated nor altered as a result of living on planets alien to their home world—when her own species headed into space they found others to whom the "wild talents" were a normal way of life.

There were the Wyverns of Warlock, whose females were age-long mistresses of thought over matter. The Thassa of Yiktor—Ziantha did not need to list them all. Part of her past training had been to study what each newly discovered world could add to the sum total of learning. What she had been able to absorb she had practiced to the height of her powers under Ogan's careful fostering. But this—

Old—old—old!

"How old?" At first Ziantha was so intent upon the problem she did not realize that question had been asked not by her own mind but by— She looked over her shoulder.

Yasa stood in the doorway, her lily scent creeping in to fill the room. At her feet Harath bobbed up and down, hopping on his clawed feet, as if so greatly excited by something that he could not remain still. His beak opened and shut in a harsh clicking.

"Yesss—" Yasa's voice was more of a hiss than usual, and Ziantha recognized that sign of controlled anger. "How old —and what isss thisss thing which isss ssso old?"

"That—" Ziantha pointed to the lump.

The Salarika moved with fluid grace, coming to stand beside where Ziantha crouched. She leaned over, staring round-eyed.

32

"For thisss you do what issss forbidden? Why, I asssk you now, why?"

Her amber-red eyes caught and held Ziantha mercilessly. Humanoid Yasa might be in general form, but there was no human type of emotion which Ziantha could detect in that long stare.

The girl wet her lower lip with her tongue. She had met so many trials this day, it was as if she were now numb. Ordinarily she would have known fear of Yasa in this mood; now she could only tell the truth, or what seemed the truth.

"I had to—"

"Sssso? What order had been given you to do thissss?"

"I—when I was in Jucundus's apartment this—this pulled me. I could not forget it. It—it made me reach for it—"

"She could be right, you know."

Just as Yasa had entered unbidden and unexpected, now Ogan appeared. "There are strong compulsions sometimes when a sensitive is at top pitch performance. Tell me"—he, too, came to stand over Ziantha—"when were you aware of this first? Before or after you read the tapes?"

"After, when I was going out of the room. It was so strong —a call I never felt before."

He nodded. "Could be so. You had the vibrations high; a thing attuned to those vibrations could respond with a summons. Where was this—in the safe?"

"No." She explained how she had seen it first, one of a number of curiosities set out on a small table.

"What isss all thisss—?" Yasa began when an imperative wave from Ogan's hand not only halted her question but turned her attention back to the artifact.

Ogan's hand now rested on Ziantha's head. She longed to jerk away, throw off that touch, light and unmenacing though it was, but submitted to it. Ogan had his own ways of detecting truth or falsehood, and she needed him more at this moment as a protection against Yasa's wrath.

"This then obsessed you until you had to apport it?" His voice was encouraging, coaxing.

"I could not get it otherwise," she returned sullenly.

"So you were able, because of this obsession, to develop powers you did not use before?"

"I had Harath to back me."

"Yesss!" Had Yasa still possessed the tail of her ancestors she might have lashed it at that moment; instead she made her voice a whip to lash with words. "Thisss one takes Harath, and with him sssshe makes trouble!" Harath snapped his beak violently as Yasa paused, as if heartily agreeing with her accusation. "Sssomewhere now in Tikil there isss a Patrol ssssensitive at alert. How long you think before Jucundusss beginsss to wonder?"

To Ziantha's surprise, Ogan smiled. She sensed that under his generally expressionless exterior he was excited, even pleased.

"Lady! Bethink you—how many dwell in that apartment where Jucundus chooses to make his headquarters? Two—three—perhaps four hundred! There are endless possibilities. If Jucundus values this thing so little as to leave it in the open, will he miss it for a while? It is true that a sensitive on patrol might well have picked up the surge of Ziantha's power. But to detect and trace it would be impossible unless he had a scan ready for action. She and Harath were right, or rather Harath was right to shut down on communication when he detected the hunter. All the sensitive can say now is that someone within the park put forth an expenditure of energy in an unusual degree. But"—Ogan looked again at Ziantha—"that you escaped was not due to any intelligence on your part, girl."

She was willing to agree. "No, it was Harath."

"Yes, Harath, who will now tell us what we have here."

"But I—" Ziantha half raised her hand in protest.

"You are of no value in the matter, not now. Have you

not already tried?" He spoke impatiently as he might to a child who was being tiresome, as he had in the past when she was younger and would not be as pliable as he wished. "Harath," he repeated coldly.

She wanted to cover the artifact with her hands, her body, hide it. It was hers—from the beginning she had known it to be hers. But she was in no condition to read it; her ill-tried experiment proved that. And she wanted to know what it was, from whence it had come, why it should exert such influence over her.

It seemed that Harath had to be coaxed. For he caught at the fluttering ends of Yasa's fringed skirt, turning his head away, only clicking his beak in a staccato of protest when Ogan ordered him to touch the lump.

Yasa folded her slender legs, gracefully joining Ziantha on the floor. She ran her fingers gently over the head of the small alien, purring soothingly, making no mind-send the girl could detect, but in some manner of her own, communicating, coaxing, bringing Harath to a better temper.

At last, with a final ruffle of beak drum, he loosed his hold on her skirt and crossed the cushions with extreme wariness, as if he fully expected an explosion to follow any touch, even through the mind alone. Squatting down, he advanced from his down-covered pocket a single tentacle, brought it over so that the tip alone just touched the artifact.

Eagerly Ziantha opened her own channel of communication, ready to pick up whatever the alien would report.

"Not early"—that was Ogan's caution. "Give us the latest reading."

Ziantha picked up a sensation of distress.

"All ways at once—much—much—" Harath's answer was a protest.

"Give us the latest," Ogan insisted.

"Hidden—deep hidden——Oheee——dark—death—" Har-

35

ath's thought was as sharp as a scream. He snatched away his tentacle as if the figure were searing hot.

"How did Jucundus get it?" It was Yasa this time who asked. "Little one, little brave one, you can see that for us. What is this precious thing?"

"A place, an old place—where death lies. Hidden, old—strange. It is cold from the long time since it was in sun and light. Death and cold. Many things around it once—a great —great lord there. No—not to see!"

He whipped the tentacle away again, into complete hiding. But he did not turn away, rather stood regarding the artifact.

Then: "It is of those you call Forerunners. The very ancient ones. And it is—was—once one of two—"

Ziantha heard a hiss which formed no word. Yasa's lips were a little apart, there was an avid glow in her large eyes.

"Well done, little one." She put out her hand as if to fondle Harath. But he turned, made his way unsteadily across the pillows to stand beside Ziantha.

"I do not know how," he reported on the open mind-send they all now shared, "but this one, she is a part of it. It is Ziantha who can find, if finding comes at all, where this once lay. Dark and cold and death." His round eyes held unblinkingly on Ziantha. She shivered as she had when she had come out of the trance of the apport. But she knew that what he said was the truth. By some curse of temperament or fortune she was linked to this ugly thing beyond all hope of freedom.

"Forerunner tomb!" Yasa held one of her girdle scent bags to her nose, sniffing in refreshment the strong odor of the powdered lily petals. "Ogan, we must discover whence Jucundus had this—"

"If he bought it, Lady, or if he brought it with him—" It was plain that Ogan was equally excited.

"What matter? Whatever a man has discovered can be

found. Do we not have more eyes and ears almost than the number of stars over us?"

"If bought, it could well be loot from a tomb already discovered," Ziantha ventured.

Yasa looked at her. "You believe that? That it is some unknown curiosity picked up perhaps at the port mart with no backtracing for its origin? It has no beauty to the eye—age alone and a link with the Forerunners would make it worthy to be displayed and cherished. Also Jucundus has pretensions to hist-test learning. He backed three survey groups on Fennis, striving to place the mound builders there. But old as those were, they were not true Forerunners, nor were they tombs. No, Jucundus kept this with him because of its history, which we must learn. Now we shall put it in safekeeping until—"

She would have taken it up. But, though her fingers scrabbled in the air, she could not touch its surface.

"Ogan! What is the matter?"

He came swiftly around the mound of cushions. After a slow study of the artifact he caught Yasa's wrist.

"Psychokinetic energy. It is charged past a point I have ever seen before. Lady, this—this thing must once have been a focus for some parapsychological use. That which gathered in it during the time it was used has now been brought to life by the power bent on it when apported. It is like mindpower itself. Unless it is discharged in some fashion, it is highly dangerous to the touch. Unless—" He turned on Ziantha. "Pick it up! At once, do you hear!"

The snap of his order made her move before she thought. Her hand closed about the lump with no difficulty. It appeared to be warm—or was that only her imagination, primed by what Ogan had just said? But if Yasa had been unable to touch it, that barrier did not hold for her.

"Psychic tie," Ogan pronounced. "Until it is fully discharged, if it ever will be, Lady, this girl is the only one who can handle it."

"Surely you can neutralize it in some manner! You have all your devices—of what good are those?" Yasa was plainly not prepared to accept his decision.

"Of this condition we have theoretical knowledge, Lady. But in a hundred planet years or more no worship object of an alien race has ever been found to be so studied. An artifact which has been the object of worship of a nation or species acquires, with every ceremony of worship, a certain residue of power. So charged, it literally becomes, as the ancient men said, god-like. There were god-kings and -queens of old who were the objects of worship by those who served them, and who were fed by the psychic energies of those who adored them. Thus they achieved the power which made them perform miracles and brought them indeed close to the all-might they professed to have."

"And you believe this to be such a god-thing?" There was a shadow of disbelief in the Salarika's voice.

"It is clearly a thing of psychic power far past the ordinary. And I tell you I dare not put it to any test I could devise, because I might destroy what it holds. We may have chanced on such a treasure as we could not have hoped to discover in a lifetime."

Perhaps it was the word "treasure" which brought the throat-purr of satisfaction from Yasa.

"But you believe that you can perhaps use it—through our cubling here—" The look she now gave Ziantha was both forgiving and approving.

"I will and can promise nothing, Lady. But with such a key I think old doors can be opened. We must start, of course, to trace its history while it was in Jucundus's possession. Whether its import was known to him in more than a general way, I greatly doubt. He does not like sensitives, as we well know. Men with secrets to hide do not. I can believe that while it was in his hands no one capable of sensing its real value and meaning could have seen it. Though it must have been aroused by apporting. Only Ziantha knew it for what it was, or felt its pull, when she passed by the table on which it lay. A combination of lucky chances, Lady. That she should be in heightened state when she first found it, so drawn to it, that she should then set it afire by using psychokinetic means to obtain it. Two factors out of the normal, reacting on it and on her in a short time, have set up a rapport we can use very well.

"Now, my girl," he spoke to Ziantha, "you will be advised to try to read this."

"I cannot!" she cried. "I tried, but I cannot! It—it was horrible."

Yasa laughed. "To teach you, cubling, not to take such grave matters on yourself. You will, however, attend to what Ogan is saying or suffer a mind-lock." She spoke lightly enough, but Ziantha had no doubt that she meant exactly what she threatened. Only the girl did not need such a threat; her fascination with the artifact had not been in any way lessened, though she had suffered enough during that one attempt to solve its mystery to know that she could not try that again—not as she felt now.

"In your guardianship then, cubling." Yasa arose. "Or perhaps in its own, if Ogan's reading of its present state continues. Meanwhile we shall take up the matter of where Jucundus first found it."

4

There was no need of any warning. Ziantha realized she had in truth condemned herself to captivity in the villa while that vast underground of spies Yasa maintained went into action. The girl had expected Ogan to show more interest though, both in her sudden development of psychokinetic powers and in the artifact. She had anticipated, with dread, hours of lab testing. And, when no such summons came, she was first relieved, then a little piqued at being so ignored. Did the parapsychologist think the artifact would continue to be so "charged" that it would defy his powers of research? Or was he only preparing stiffer tests?

Whatever the cause of her semi-imprisonment, Ziantha became more and more uneasy as the hours, and then the days, wore on. There were amusement and information tapes in plenty to draw upon, and the tri-dee casts from Tikil on her screen if she cared to tune them in. But all the various things with which she had filled waiting hours before no longer had the power to hold her attention.

After she made two tangles in the belt she was knotting by a process Yasa's Salarika maid had taught her, and found that she could not concentrate on a tape of Forerunner "history" she had in the reader, she gave up on the morning of the third day. Sitting in the deep window-sill lounge, she looked out into the garden, which was a type of jungle, carefully maintained in that state to ensure Yasa's privacy.

Forerunners—there were many different kinds, civilizations, species— Not even the Zacathans—those reptilian-evolved, very long-lived Hist-techneers and archaeologists of the galaxy—had ever been able to chart them all. Her own species was late come to the stars, springing from a small system on the very fringe of this galaxy, that which contained the fabled Terra of Sol. Waves of emigration and settlement had gone forth from that planet—some fleeing wars at home, some questing for adventure and new beginnings. They had found new worlds—some of them—and in turn those worlds altered, changed the settlers through generations. New suns, different trace elements in soil, air, food, had brought about mutations. There was still a legendary Terran "norm," but she had yet to meet a single person who directly matched it. There were "giants" compared to the given height, as well as "dwarfs." Skin color, hair hue or lack of hair, number of digits, ability or limitation of sight, hearing, the rest of the senses, all these characteristics existed in a vast number of gradations and differences. To realize that, one need only visit the Dipple, where the sweepings of the civilizations of half a hundred planets had been dropped, or walk the streets of Tikil with an intent of measuring those differences.

And if the Terrans had been so modified and altered by their spread to the stars, then those earlier races they called the Forerunners must have suffered in their time the same changes. But they had left behind them enigmatic traces of their passing. When that passing had resulted from titanic conflicts, one found "burned-off" worlds reduced to such cinders as to remain horror monuments to deadly fury. However, there were other planets where wondering men found ruins, tombs, even installations which could still work after what, a million years of planet time?

Each find usually added a new question, did not answer many. For those who studied the discoveries could not string together a quarter of such remains into a pattern they could recognize as belonging to any one civilization or people. Here and there a legend collected by the patient netting of the Zacathans from star to star gave a name—of a race? A ruler? Often they were not even sure. And so, for example, the pillar city on Archon IV and two ports on Mochican and Wotan were tentatively linked as "Zaati" because of some similar carvings.

The hopes were always for the discovery of some storehouse of knowledge, of tapes, or of records that could enlighten a little. Two years ago there had come the discovery of a world which was a single huge city, the apex of one of the civilizations of star-traveling races. That was being explored now.

Ziantha brushed her hand across her forehead. She had always been interested in Forerunners. But now— She glanced over her shoulder to that box on the table. When Yasa had left the artifact in her keeping she had emptied her lockbox and had bundled the lump, still wrapped in the scarf she had put about it, into the box and had not looked at it since. But neither had she been able to put it out of mind.

A ring with a strange and deadly gem stone had been the key to the city-world. The story of that quest had been told and retold on tri-dee casts a thousand times. What had she found? Another key—to open what door and where?

Korwar had its own ancient mystery—Ruhkarv. That was a maze of underground ways built by a people, or entities, totally alien. It was a wicked trap, so the Rangers of the Wild had force-walled it against penetration. No one knew who had dug the ways of Ruhkarv, whether it was to be named "city" or "hive," or whether it was a fort, an indwelling, or a way-station for alien off-worlders.

Slowly Ziantha arose, moving against her will, compelled by the force that the artifact could exert. She shrank from what the box held, yet she picked it up and brought it back into the shaft of strong sunlight which beat through the window, as if something in that natural light could disarm what she held, render it her captive rather than allow her to remain in its thrall.

Drawing out the wrapped lump, she set it in the sun, plucked at the folds of scarf covering it until they fell away. It was dull, ugly; it could have been the result of a child's attempt at modeling the clay gouged from some riverbank. There was certainly nothing about it that hinted at any higher star-reaching, far ranging civilization—very primitive.

Greatly daring, Ziantha put forth a hand, touched. But this time there was no answering flare of energy. Ogan's theory that the act of apporting might have charged it—was she now proving the truth of that? The girl began to run her finger back and forth, with more confidence, across the upper portion, where there should have been a head.

Though the lump seemed rough to the eye, to the touch it was smooth. And she picked up only a faint flicker of something—

Suddenly Ziantha caught it up between her palms, pressed thumbs on the top, four fingers underneath, and gave a quick twist of the right wrist, wrenching at the lump. She did not know why, only this she must do.

The deceptively rough-looking shell moved at her action. Half of it turned away from her. It did not crumble but parted evenly in two as if it were a box.

Within was a nest of silver, glittering thread coiled about and about, plainly designed to protect an inner core. Ziantha set the half of the artifact which held this on the window sill. She was cautious enough not to touch the thread with her bare fingers. Instead she brought from the table a long-hafted spoon she had used to stir a glass of fal-berry juice.

Reversing this, she began to probe the puff of thread warily, pushing in until she cleared a peephole. The sun reached beyond the brilliant sparks awakened from the spun filaments and touched what she had uncovered, bringing a wink of blue-green.

An oval stone lay there—a gem she was sure, though she did not recognize it by color alone. It was about half the length of her thumb and cut smoothly cabochon, not faceted. She turned her head quickly, pushing the covering back over it, knowing in that instant it had almost entranced her.

Crystallomancy was one of the oldest ways of inducing clairvoyance. Focusing on a globe wrought of some clear stone or gem brought the sensitive to the point where the power was released. Ogan was right about such objects. When in long use they built up psychic energy within them. This was what she had—a gazing crystal which had been used for a long time to release talent.

As swiftly as she could Ziantha set the two halves of the lump together, closed it with a counter twist. She studied its surface. There was no sign of that seam, not the slightest indication it could be opened. With a sigh of relief she re-wrapped it and stowed it in the box. Only when that was locked away did she relax.

If she had taken it, used it as it was meant to be used, what would she have seen? The death and dark that it had broadcast through its outer protection? She had no intention of trying to find out, nor did she intend to let Ogan or Yasa know of this second discovery. That they would set her to using the stone she did not doubt. And she dared not—

She had time to school herself a mind-protection, though she doubted whether she would be able to hold that if Ogan suspected. However, it seemed that events beyond the villa were in her favor. For before midmorning she was summoned to Yasa's chamber, passing through the cloud of perfumed vapor to find the Salarika veep with a man she knew to be one of the traveling coordinators of the Guild.

He scrutinized Ziantha coldly, as if she were not a person but a tool—or weapon—and he were judging her effectiveness. In Yasa Ziantha detected no sign of unease, though the upper grades of the Guild were perilous to those who aspired to gain them. Advancement went largely by assassination. An "erase" could be ordered for any veep who was either considered "unsafe," or who stood in the path of some ambitious underling.

When a check was run by one of the coordinators, there was always a question of trouble. But if Yasa had any reservations concerning this visit, no human would be able to read that from her, any more than a detect could ensnare her thoughts when she wished to retire behind her own alien "cover." Now she watched Ziantha with a lazy, unblinking stare, but on her knee sat Harath, his eyes closed as if he were asleep. Ziantha, seeing him, was instantly warned. She had been long enough in this household to mark any deviation from the routine as a battle signal and to take up her part of the defense.

Yasa was *not* as easy as she seemed, or Harath would not be playing the pet role. He had been ordered to pick up any leakage from the visitor's mind-lock. Which meant that Yasa would give no information to this coordinator, and Ziantha must be very careful what she herself said. Since the artifact was the main concern at present, that, above all, must be secret.

She had only a moment or two to grasp this, to prepare a defense, when Yasa waved a hand in her direction.

"This is the sensitive who gathered the tape readings, Mackry. You asked to see her; she is here."

He was a large man, once well-muscled and imposing-looking, now a little jowly, a little too paunchy. The spacer's uniform he wore, with a captain's wings, fit a little too tight. Either it had not been tailored for him, or he had put it aside for some time and now found it irksome. On his chin was a small beard, smoothed and stiffened to curl out in an imperious point. But the rest of his face was smooth, dark red in color; his head was shaved bare and then overlaid with a filigree of silver in swirls, as one might wear a very tight cap.

His eyes were deeply sunken, or perhaps it was the puffiness of his cheeks which made them appear so, and his brows had been treated to stand out in points to match his beard. Those eyes, for all their retreat behind flesh and hair, were very hard and bright, reminding Ziantha unwillingly of the glitter of that thread which nested the seeing gem, a memory she hastily buried.

He grunted, perhaps an acknowledgment to Yasa's half introduction. Then he launched into a sharp questioning of Ziantha concerning her visit to Jucundus's apartment, though he, of course, did not inquire what had been on the tapes, since Ogan had erased that. He took her step by step through the whole foray from the moment the palm lock on the door had yielded, to the end of her journey on her return to the villa. Having Yasa's unspoken warning, the girl omitted all reference to the artifact and the subsequent apporting of it.

When she had finished, and there had not been the slightest change in Yasa's expression to signal either that she was correctly following subtle directions, or making perhaps a totally irredeemable mistake, Mackry grunted again. Yasa uncurled from her usual lounging position.

"You see. Ogan checked with every scanner. It is exactly as we reported, gentle homo. There was no possible hint of detection."

"So it would seem. But the city is hot, blazing hot, I tell you! In some way that heat is tied to Jucundus. But that has-been had not made a single move to suggest that he knows his microrecords were scanned. They have a sensitive out, sniffing hard. You have kept this one"—again he regarded Ziantha, to her rising irritation, with a look that relegated her to the status of tool—"under wraps?"

"You can ask." Yasa yawned daintily. "She is here, and has been here. Our detection devices have not traced any mind-scan as a probe. With Ogan's lab here do you think such would go undetected?"

46

"Ogan!" He made that name into a snort, as if he classed the parapsychologist with Ziantha. "Well, you cannot keep her here—not now. So far our plans concerning Jucundus are going well; we want no interference. Get her off-world at once!"

Yasa yawned again. "It is near time for my leave. And I have an excellent excuse to go and visit the Romstk trading post. She shall go with my household."

"Agreed. You shall be told when to return." With no further word he stalked from the room, his rudeness deliberate, Ziantha knew. Her guess was confirmed when she looked at Yasa.

The feline contoured face of the Salarika was expressionless as far as the human eye could tell, except that the alien's lips were drawn very tight against her teeth, showing the sharp white points of what in her ancestors had been tearing, death-dealing fangs.

"Mackry," Yasa observed in a thoughtful tone, her voice almost as emotionless as she could make her features, "takes his missions with a seriousness that suggests he sees before him a flight of stairs climbing to heights. Oftentimes when one's attention is fixed too far ahead and at the wrong angle, one can trip over a crevice before one's very feet. But in so much does he serve our purpose—we needed a reason to take off from Korwar without question from those using Mackry —though he does not reckon the truth that he is my servant here, rather than master."

"You have learned something?" Ziantha asked.

Yasa purred. "Naturally, cubling. When Yasa tells eyes to see, ears to listen, noses to sniff, they obey. We know the general direction from which came Jucundus's toy. Now we go in search of those who make it their mission in life to learn what is unknown or long forgotten. We go to Waystar."

Waystar! Ziantha had heard of it all her short life. It was considered a legend by most of the star rovers, but it existed, as all the Guild knew well, though perhaps only a handful of a handful among them even guessed in what part of the galaxy it was located. It served the Guild in some respects, but it was not a possession of the veeps of the underworld as were some other secret bases.

Long before the Guild came into power, before the first of the Terrans felt their way along unmapped stellar roads, Waystar had been. It was a port of outlaws, a rendezvous for space pirates when piracy existed. Now it was a meeting place for Jacks, those outlaws who raided sparsely settled planets and installations, and for the Guildmen, who bought the loot from such raids, or hired Jacks at times to carry out some ship plan of their own.

According to the stories, it had once been a space station located in a system now so old its planets were cinders in orbit around an almost dead red dwarf sun. If it were as old as the worlds it companied, or even as old as the life that had once ruled them, it was beyond any reckoning of age by those who now used it. It had, however, in recorded time, such a dark history as to overshadow all speculation. Going to Waystar was like saying one planned to venture into the bowels of Ruhkarv, with perhaps as good a reason to expect the worst thereafter.

"This Mackry—if we go to Waystar—" Ziantha ventured. Though the Guild did not rule there, their influence would weigh deeply enough so Yasa might be found to be playing traitor. What would happen then? When a veep fell, his or her personal following were also swept away, unless they were extraordinarily fortunate or had secret ties with the one or ones who brought about that downfall.

Yasa smoothed Harath's downy head, uttered a sound amazingly like the snapping of the creature's beak.

"Mackry is one who runs hither and thither with messages, is that not so, my soft one?" she asked Harath aloud.

His mind-send was clear. "He tries to find something with

48

which he can cause trouble for you. So far his search has brought nothing. He believes his detect shields him." There was such a strong note of scorn in that beaming that Ziantha was startled into a question of her own.

"It does not?"

Harath turned his head to look directly at her. Though that seemed an impossible angle for flesh and bone to endure, he held so, his huge eyes unblinking. "Harath can read." Again he beak-clicked scornfully.

Ziantha had not realized that the alien could penetrate the mind-seals worn as a matter of course by Guildmen. She was so enured to the marvels of their techs that she accepted as a fact that such a shield could not be pierced by normal means. But then, of course, Harath was not "normal" by her species' standards at all.

Then Yasa did have a guard when Harath was with her. Doubtless he could have relayed to the Salarika every thought passing through Mackry's mind. Or Ziantha's mind—! The stone! No, do not think of that! The trouble was when there was something not to be brought to the readable fore of one's mind, that is the very thought which haunted one. Something else— Waystar—think of Waystar—

Again the Salarika purred. "Harath reads well." There was warm approval not comment. "And there are those at Waystar before whom, for all his ambition, Mackry would dwindle until he was smaller than our Harath is in body, as he is already smaller in talent and courage."

"One has to reach Waystar to evoke the backing of such," Ziantha found the courage to point out.

"One need not put obvious truths into words, cubling. However we have not been idle. Plans were made before Mackry arrived to provide us with cover. But this will not be a luxurious voyage. We must travel in voyage-sleep and a sealed cabin."

Ziantha wished she dare refuse, though there could not

49

ever be a chance for her to set her will against that of the Salarika. Voyage-sleep and a sealed cabin was primitive travel indeed in these days, generations after the first ships traveled with their crews and passengers in frozen sleep, not knowing if they would ever awaken again. She thought now that perhaps it was not the ruggedness of the accommodations which might force this now ancient process on them, but perhaps the secrecy of Yasa's plan.

But she was not given much time to worry about possibilities, because by dusk one of Yasa's private flitters had brought them to the airport where they were escorted on board an inner world liner. Only they did not remain there. For they had no more than stepped within the cabin assigned to them before Yasa whipped two hooded cloaks from her top luggage case. So with distort outer garments they made a circuitous way along empty corridors to a lower hatch and, covered by the dusk and the distorts, swung down to ground level again on a luggage lift.

In spite of her cloak, Ziantha felt vulnerable as she scurried after Yasa across the edge of the landing field and into the shadows. Thus they came to that end of the port where few passenger ships ever sat down, which was reserved for Free Traders and lesser transports. Yasa, without hesitation, seeming to know very well what she sought, caught at Ziantha's hand and urged her to a faster pace to reach the space-scoured side of a transport on which the name and emblem was so badly worn that in this limited light the girl could make out neither symbol.

The landing ramp was out, but there was no crewman on guard at either end. Again Yasa did not hesitate, but, drawing the girl with her, hurried up into the ship. They met no one. It might have been totally deserted; Ziantha decided there must have been orders given that they not be observed entering.

Yasa climbed three levels, bringing them not far above the

cargo holds. Here was an open door which they entered, Yasa closing it quickly behind them.

"Pleasant voyaging, gentle fems." Ogan leaned against the wall. He looked oddly out of place in a drab uniform of a workman, as he stood guard over two long, narrow chests. Ziantha could not subdue the shiver which ran through her as she threw off the cloak and looked at those, knowing well what ordeal lay before her now. In spite of all that man had learned to make space flight safe, there were always failures, and she had never been off-world that she could remember. Though, of course, like all those in the Dipple, she had originally come to Korwar from some war-swept planet.

"It has gone well so far." Yasa folded their cloaks small, made pillows of them she stowed in the boxes. "Ziantha, you have the artifact—give it here."

Because she had no reason to defy that, the girl handed over the container for the lump, which she had held tightly to her during their flight across the port. Yasa stood for a moment with it in her hands. If she had intended to open it, to assure herself their prize was within, she did not do so. Instead she set it with extra care beside one of those cloak-pillows.

Ogan smiled. "How perceptive of you, Lady. Naturally if there is any relation between voyage-sleep and trance it should help. Now, Ziantha, in with you, and if our small mystery can answer any questions while you sleep, you can report it later."

Ziantha shrank back against the bulkhead. To sleep with that promise of dark and death so close? She could not! Ogan did not know what he suggested. But he probably did, and did not care. Her talent was of value to the Guild, yes, but she was certain that this was not a Guild operation—that Yasa and Ogan were planning a foray of their own. And in such she would only be useful if she could produce results.

She had stepped completely out of any safety she might have known, and there was no turning back, no way to run.

"Come, come!" Ogan put out his hand. "Let us have no child's nonsense. You have been hypnoed before—it is nothing. And think what a tale you may have to tell us later!"

In those close quarters she could not even dodge. He caught her wrists in a grip which brought a gasp from her, pulled her arm out and pressed the injector to her flesh below the elbow. Still holding her, he pulled her to the box. She climbed in numbly, lay down with her head pillowed on the folded cloak. The sides and bottom were well padded, could even be called comfortable, if one did not know the future. Beside her head was the box; she would not allow her eyes to stray in that direction.

"Good. Now you see it is all very simple, not at all painful or frightening. Look here, Ziantha—just as you have done before—before—before—" He repeated the word over and over in a dull even-toned voice as she stared, because she had to, at a swinging disk in his fingers. She had no will left, no defense—

"Before—" The word was gone; she slept.

5

Ziantha had to use all her control to keep from cowering flat on the landing stage with her suited body. Overhead (if there could be "over" or "under" in space) was a threatening mass. They had slept, for how long she never knew, and then awakened, to transfer to another ship which had brought them to the outer ring and through the concealing barrier which protected Waystar.

Such a barrier as perhaps a writer of fantasy tri-dees might have conceived—that was Waystar's first defense. For it was a mass of derelicts and parts of derelicts, as if a giant fleet of some great stellar confederacy had been wrecked by deliberate intent, brought here by traction beams, and wielded and tied to form a jagged cover about the station.

Beyond that mass of tortured metal was a stretch of free space, which was reached by traversing a "tunnel" through the wreckage. Centering that was a station which had plainly been the result of intelligent planning and construction. At either end was a landing stage and the rest was encased in a crystalline surface pitted and mended many times. But to land on one of those stages and see the massive roofing of twisted metal overhead was to produce in one, Ziantha thought, the sensation of being under a hammer about to descend. That it had not closed upon the fragile-seeming station in all the generations it had been in position did not somehow reassure her in the least.

Even once Yasa had drawn her into the entrance lock, the

memory of that weight around the station was daunting. To the girl's surprise there was a weak gravity within, though how that was maintained she never discovered.

The center was hollow, completely surrounded by corridors and balconies. A greenish light, giving the most unhealthy and unpleasant cast to the faces of the inhabitants, diffused from the walls. And those inhabitants were a mixed lot— X-Tee aliens equaling humanoids in number. In the few moments it took them to leave the lock and traverse a portion of one way, Ziantha saw even more outré forms than she had ever viewed on Korwar, which was famous for being the crossroads of many stellar lines.

The gravity was so weak that it was necessary to hold to bars set into the walls, and there were curved rods with handholds to rise and descend to the various levels. However, Yasa apparently knew the way, traveling at a brisk speed toward one of the upper levels.

Here were very faint tracings of patterns which might once have been painted on the walls, perhaps by those who fashioned this station long before the coming of Ziantha's kind into space. But these were so dimmed that one could make little sense of them; a geometric angle, a curve here and there, was all that could be traced.

They came to a door guarded by a human in space leather, one of the forbidden lasers on his hip, its butt near his hand. But at the sight of Yasa he stepped aside and let them enter. The room beyond was such a crowded space that there was too much to sort out in the first glance, or even the fifth.

The furnishings had apparently been gathered with no thought of harmony; there were pieces which could have been ripped from half a hundred plundered ships. Some were intended for the use of humans, others for alien accommodation. What they had in common was a display of ornate riches (or what had once been that, for they were now battered and dingy).

Stretched at length in the midst of this storehouse of stolen goods was the veep Yasa had chosen to consult about the artifact. He snapped his fingers as they entered and a green-skinned Wyvern male scuttled forward to push and pull out two hassocks for their seating. But the veep did not rise in greeting, only lifted his hand in Yasa's direction in a slight salute.

The Salarika, who on Korwar was accorded the full deference for not only her sex but her standing in the Guild, apparently here was not worthy of formality. But if she were piqued by this reception, she showed no sign of it.

This veep, like his quarters, was a mixture of both magnificence and slovenly disorder. Unlike many beings they had passed outside, he showed almost pure Terran descent in his person, though his clothing was barbaric. Like the heads of mercenaries of some centuries earlier, his skull was shaved save for an upstanding roach of black hair, the stiffness of which was reinforced by a band of green-gold metal. And from this circlet a fine koro stone depended, to rest against his forehead.

His skin was the brown of a spaceman, and there were purposely shaped scars running from the corner of each eye to his chin on either side of his mouth, giving his features a cruel frame, as if living flesh had been carved to produce a mask meant to terrify.

Breech-legging boots of a very soft and pliable fur—white with a ripple pattern—covered him to the waist. Above that was the full-dress tunic of a Patrol Admiral, black-silver, with all the be-gemmed stars and decorations such an officer was entitled to wear. The sleeves had been cut away. On his bare arms, just below his elbows, were cuff bracelets of iridium, one thickly set with Terran rubies, the other with rows of vivid blue-and-green stones.

There was a tray resting across his thighs, but it held no dishes. Instead there was something there so exquisitely beautiful that it was totally out of place in this barbaric setting. It was a miniature garden, with tiny trees, bushes, and a lake in which a minute boat sailed for an island that was a single mountain of rock. Ziantha's attention followed it as the Wyvern carried it to a table.

The veep spoke Basic in an educated voice that did not match his pirate chieftain's dress.

"My garden, gentle fem. This is the best one can do on Waystar, where nothing will grow. But this is of spice wood, with scented water for its lake. One can hold it, close the eyes, and wander in one's imagination—a substitute for the real, but it must serve."

Yasa was holding one of her scent bags to her nose, no longer able to do without the reviving stimulation her species needed. The veep smiled, the scars rendering that stretch of lips no more attractive than the grimace of a night demon would have been.

"My apologies, gentle fem. Waystar is rich in many things—including odors, but not of the kind your people delight in. So let us return to business before you discover you can no longer get any reviving sniffs from your supply of lily petals. Your message was received. Perhaps I can serve you, perhaps not—there are difficulties, and arrangements." Again he smiled.

Yasa's smile matched his, with some of the same merciless quality in it. "Of a truth, how could it be otherwise? I am prepared, Sreng, to discuss it at length."

For a moment there was silence as their eyes met. Ziantha knew that any bargaining would be a fiercely fought action. But, since they needed each other, terms would eventually be met. The Salarika had not given her much information as to what they sought here at Waystar, save to say that the riddle of where the artifact might have come from would be best answered by those she could meet there.

"We have used the computer to reckon the coordinates

56

which you sent us," he said. Perhaps Yasa's recognition of the need for bargaining satisfied Sreng. "There is a possible mapping. What do you do now?"

Yasa looked to Ziantha. "We shall search—"

Ziantha's hands tightened on the box she held. She knew what Yasa meant, but she mistrusted her own powers for this; she was not trained to it. What if she could not deliver? Did this Sreng have some sensitive of his own who would then take over? But that would mean relinquishing the box's contents to another, and she believed that Yasa would consent to that only on direst necessity.

The technique of such a search was age old, known to every sensitive. But not all had the talent to use it effectively. And, while she knew it had been applied to planet maps, could it be so used on a star map? She hoped that Yasa did not expect too much, and that they might lose advantage to this veep because she, Ziantha, could not search.

"We need rest, a little," Yasa said now with a certain note of authority in her voice which argued that she considered herself, even in Waystar, to be also a veep whose well-being was to be reckoned on.

"Your desire is my wish—" He made a mockery of that formal reply. "SSssfani will show you to quarters, which, though most rough compared to your own holding, gentle fem, are unfortunately the best we can offer. When you are ready, you have only to send word and we shall to work."

The Wyvern led them farther along the same corridor to a chamber furnished with the same looted jumble. When he had departed Yasa turned briskly to the girl.

"Rest you well, cubling. It now lies on you—" As she spoke her hands moved under the edge of her shoulder scarf in a complicated pattern. Ziantha read the signals.

Snooper rays! Of course in such a place as this those were to be suspected. She probably dared not even try mind-touch —they would be surrounded by more than one type of detect.

"I shall do my best, Lady." She settled on an eazi-rest, which adjusted to her comfort more smoothly than she expected from its battered appearance. Yasa had gone to the food server on the wall and was fingering the dial as she read its code. She sniffed.

"Limited, but at least it will keep life in our bodies—all synthetics. Not much better than E-rations." She seemed only too willing to give her opinion, especially if their host was listening.

Ziantha made do with the tube of concentrate which was Yasa's selection. It was highly nourishing, she knew, even if there was a flatness of taste. She lay back in the eazi-rest. One part of her dreaded the coming test; another wanted it to happen as soon as possible, to learn if it would be success or failure. But here she must follow Yasa's lead. She was supposed to be resting, though her anticipation would not allow that.

There was something else. As she lay back and closed her eyes, clearing her mind, building up her psychic energy, she was aware of a—stirring. In no other way could she describe that odd, disquieting feeling that nibbled at the edge of her inner awareness.

A little alarmed, Ziantha concentrated on that area of faint disturbance. The sensation came and went like the lightest of nudges. Now she was sure that it was not born from some layer of her own consciousness. She was being scanned! Though the touch was so faint she could not hope to trace it.

But perhaps Sreng had a sensitive trying her. Only this— Ziantha could not push away the thought that that touch was not trying to gauge her strength of talent— It was—

Confused, she raised her defenses. What *had* she sensed in that moment or two? Mind-touch. However not with the force she expected from a test. Rather as if some questing net had been thrown over Waystar, or this portion of it, merely to see if there was another sensitive within range.

Ziantha tried to be logical. Sreng would have known in advance who and what she was. Yasa would have made no secret of it. This could be some rival of the veep, intent on gaining knowledge—it could be a Guild representative checking on Yasa. Whoever it was, she believed it the enemy.

But she had so little to give Yasa in confirmation of what she had felt. Best keep quiet until she was entirely sure that she had been touched. Only, keep her own defenses up from now on.

The girl was still on the alert when they returned to Sreng's crowded room, where there was now a difference. Some of the furniture had been ruthlessly cleared away to make room for a table on which was spread a star map. To Ziantha it had little meaning, since she was no astrogator. But that would argue in her behalf if she received any message from the artifact. Concentrating on the lump, even as she unboxed and held it between her hands, she moved it out to hold over the map, beginning a slow progress from left corner to right. So far there was nothing in return.

She had covered nearly three quarters of the map when there was a change. It was as if the lump warmed to life. From it came a sharp mental picture, so very clear that she felt as if what she saw existed, that she could reach out and touch a rock, a wind-blown bush!

"Rocks—" she spoke without knowing she did so until she heard her own voice. "There are trees, a road—yes, a road— it leads to— No!" She might have hurled the lump from her at that moment, but it was as if her own flesh were fastened to its surface and she could not free herself from that touch any more than she could free herself from the cloud of terror that entrapped her, until that was all the world and there was nothing else. She thought she screamed—cried for help!

The cloak of fear fell away, leaving her sobbing, so shaken

she was weak and would have fallen had Yasa not supported her.

"Death—death! Death in the dark. In the tomb with Turan—death!"

Who was Turan? Now she could not remember. She must not! Sreng leaned over the table to make quick marks on the map. The lump was free now in her hold. She thrust it away from her so that it slid along the map, would have fallen to the floor had not Sreng caught it, keeping his hand upon it as he looked at them.

"A tomb as you guessed, gentle fem," he spoke to Yasa. "Dare we hope unlooted? At least this system is unknown according to our records. Which is a good sign. What else have you learned, girl? This piece has been in your keeping; surely you have picked up more."

Dumbly Ziantha shook her head. She was still shaking from the aftermath of that panic.

"It is death—death waiting—" she said dully.

"Death waits in every tomb," commented Yasa. "But whatever was there to frighten has long since gone. This is true Forerunner."

"Which in no way certifies that all danger has been eradicated by time," was Sreng's answer. "Though the rewards may be beyond price, the danger can be great. Sometimes there are traps. One may find a Scroll of Shlan or be crushed by an ingenious deadfall."

Yasa smiled. "Does not one each day play a game of chance? I did not come here to listen to warn-offs, nor are you one to sit and give them, Sreng—unless time has softened you. You speak of Shlan—that emperor who was buried with the greatest art treasure of his time encasing his body as a shroud. And that is only one of the finds that has been made. What of Var, and Llanfer, and the Gardens of Arzor, the whole planet of Limbo? Do I need to list the others? This is

60

a chance to hunt in a section where no one else has yet searched."

Sreng looked at the chart. "At least not yet," he said. "If Jucundus—"

Yasa interrupted him. "He has made no move, we know that. But it may be a matter of time. He needs only to have a psychometric reading. However"—she smiled again—"if he has not, he cannot now."

"You"—the veep turned to Ziantha—"this Turan you babbled of, who was he?"

She did not hold that memory. "It is a name, no more."

His stare did not change, but she believed he thought she was lying. What would happen now? Would he put her under a scanner? She was so afraid, she could not control the tremor in her hands, waiting for that fate to come. But he said nothing, instead looked again at the lump, rubbing one finger across its back.

Ziantha stiffened. Had he detected the seam? Would he now open it? Instead, he gave the artifact a push in her direction.

"Keep it with you, girl. I am told the power of these things increases if they continue in a sensitive's hold. We shall need your direction again. It is well"—he spoke now to Yasa— "this is worth the use of a ship. Iuban is in orbit. He had only an abortive raid on Fenris and is under obligation to me for supplies. A class D Free Trader convert. Rough travel, gentle fems—"

"Deep sleep will answer that," Yasa returned. "We have no wish to be cabin passengers on such a ship. You will time-lock our sleep boxes."

"How wise of you, gentle fem," his menace-smile showed two teeth almost as fanglike as Yasa's own. "Deep sleep and time locks—set so myself. Iuban is *my* man, however." Those last words were a warning which Yasa accepted with a surface good humor. To Ziantha the Salarika veep seemed uncommonly trusting. But perhaps here she could do no more than accept Sreng's arrangements.

Where was Ogan? Since their transfer to the shuttle which had brought them to Waystar after their first awakening, they had seen nothing of him. But that he was to be ruled out of this venture, Ziantha did not believe.

The rest of their stay on Waystar was short, and they kept to the chamber Sreng had assigned them. Twice more Ziantha was aware of that illusive scan. It had first alarmed her, but later she sought it, her curiosity aroused. It was not mechanically induced, of that she was certain. The touch was that of a living entity—Ogan? But the wave length seemed different. And she thought it was not seeking her so much as pursuing some purpose of its own.

They joined Iuban's ship and were again boxed for the voyage. From what Ziantha had seen of the ship and its crew, to be so sealed from them was an excellent choice. Once more she prepared to sleep away time with the lump beside her. If she had dreamed any dreams induced by its proximity before, she had not remembered them, and this second time she did not fear the long sleep.

When they were aroused, Iuban's ship was already in orbit around a planet, and he summoned Yasa and Ziantha to the control cabin to watch through the visa-screen the changing view of the world below.

"Where do we set down, gentle fem?" he asked harshly.

He was young, or young seeming, for his command, and not unhandsome—until one saw the dead chill of his eyes, which made him the semblance of a man without warmth or emotion. Perhaps he was of mutation or crossbreed, for his hands were six-fingered and his ears mere holes. By the way his space tunic fitted Ziantha guessed that he had other body peculiarities.

It was plain that he had tight command of his motley crew. And it was also apparent that he united in his person the

62

ruthlessness of a top-rated Jack captain with an intelligence that might differ in part from the Terran but in its own way was of a high level.

Yasa put her hand on Ziantha's arm. "Where?" she asked the girl. "Have you any guide?"

As Ziantha hesitated, unable to answer, Iuban uttered an impatient sound. Then he added:

"We have neither time, manpower, nor supplies, gentle fem, to search the whole planet. Besides"—he touched a button and the scene on the visa-screen sharpened—"that's no territory to search. By the looks, it's been near to a burn-off down there."

Ziantha had seen in the video-history tapes the records of planets burned off, not only in war, but in some ancient disaster. Some were cinder balls; on others, mutant and ofttimes radioactive vegetation straggled, attempting to keep a few forms of life in the pockets between churned and twisted swaths of soil and recooled molten rock.

From the picture now flitting before her as the ship swung in orbit, she could see that some disaster, either manmade or a vast convulsion of nature, had struck this unknown world. There were great, deep-riven chasms, their rims knife-sharp; stretches of what could be only deserts, with, at great intervals, some touch of color suggesting vegetation. They were over a sea now, one manifestly shrunken to half its former size.

But she had no guide—

Fool! There was Singakok. It was as if a ripple had crossed the screen. She saw a city, rich land around it. Why, she could easily distinguish the Tower of Vut, long avenues, the—

"There!"

But even as she cried that aloud, Singakok was gone. There was only rock and more rock. Ziantha shook her head. Singakok—Vut—the avenues—from whence had come those names? How had she seen a city, known it as if she had

63

walked its pavements all her life? They had asked her and she had seen it, as if it were real! Yet it could not have been.

Iuban no longer gave her any attention. He spoke to the astro-navigator. "Got it?"

"Within measurable error, yes."

She must tell them, not let them land because of that weird double flash of sight. Then prudence argued that she leave well enough alone. It might be that the artifact had given her vision of something which had once existed on that site, and, since they had picked up nothing else of any promise, that was as good a place as any to begin looking. Yet she was uneasy at Iuban's quick acceptance, and of what might happen should her suggestion prove to be wrong.

They strapped down for a landing that had to be carefully plotted in that rough country. Nor did they stir from their places until the readings on atmosphere and the like came through. For all its destroyed surface, it registered Arth-type One, and they would be able to explore without helmets and breathing equipment.

But they had landed close to evening and Yasa and Iuban agreed not to explore until morning. He turned his own cabin over to the women, staying in the control section above. When they were alone Ziantha dared to make plain her fear.

"This may not be what you wish—" she said in a half-whisper, not knowing if some listening device could be now turned on them.

"What made you select it then?" Yasa wanted to know.

Ziantha tried to describe those moments when the picture of Singakok had flowed across the screen, a city which seemingly no longer existed.

"Singakok, Vut," Yasa repeated the names.

"That is the closest I can say them," the girl said. "They are from another language—not Basic."

"Describe this city, try to fix it in your mind," Yasa ordered.

Detail by detail Ziantha strove to remember that fleeting

picture. And she found that the harder she tried to remember, the more points came clearer in her mind. As if even now she could "see" what she strove to describe.

"I think you have had a true seeing," Yasa commented. "When Ogan arrives, we can—if we have not by then located any trace—entrance you for a far-seeking reading."

"Then Ogan comes?"

"Cubling, did you think that I throw away any advantage blindly? We needed Sreng's computer records. In their way they are more complete than even those of Survey, since they deal with sections of the starways even the Survey Scouts have not fully pioneered. But to then meekly make a pact with Waystar—no, that is not what any but a fool would do! Ogan will have traced us. He brings with him those sworn to me alone. Whatever treachery Sreng contemplates through Iuban and such trash will not avail. Now listen well—if we find traces of your city tomorrow, well and good. We must keep Iuban tail down here until Ogan arrives. But play your guiding well; delay all you can—try not to bring us to this tomb of Turan until we do have reinforcements of our own."

Tomb of Turan—the words rang in Ziantha's mind. There was a stir deep down—not of memory (how could it be memory?) but of intense fear. She was instantly aware.

6

"Ziantha!"

Not a spoken call to bring her so out of sleep. No, this was a stir within her mind, though it awoke her so she lay in the cramped berth looking into the dark—listening—

"Ziantha?"

She had not been dreaming then. Ogan? She sent out a mind-seek before she thought of the danger that Iuban might be equipped with some Guild device to pick up and register such activity.

"Harath!" Her recognition of the mental force meeting hers was instantaneous and left her bewildered. But Harath must be back on Korwar. Ogan surely had not brought the alien on this foray. And there was no possible method by which mind-touch could cross the stellar distance between this unknown planet and Korwar.

"What—?" Questions crowded. But the beaming of the other overrode all her own thoughts with the intensity of the message he would deliver.

"Think—think of me! We must have a reference point."

Allies after all—this was what Yasa had warned of—her following must be guided in. Obediently Ziantha produced a mental picture of Harath, held that with all the strength she could summon, pushing aside her curiosity in the need for providing a beacon guide to those the Salarika expected.

As suddenly as a clap of hands a new message came. "It is well."

She was cut off by the rise of Harath's mind shield. Having what he needed, the alien had severed connections. And Ziantha knew of old that communication could not be renewed without his cooperation.

The girl turned her head. Through the dim night light she could see Yasa curled up opposite her, hear the soft regularity of her breathing. The Salarika was asleep. Should she wake her, tell her Ogan was on the way?

But Harath—how had he come into this? No, she would wait until she was sure. Twice before morning she mind-called. But if the alien was still within beam, he would not answer, and she had to accept that.

They were roused early, and Ziantha, fearful of some snooper, decided to wait until they were away from the ship before she relayed her news. Iuban had suited up too, plainly prepared to go with them. And she must be most careful about awakening any suspicion.

The Jack captain eyed her while she buckled on belt with ration pouch and water carrier as if he would like to have added a leash to keep her to his hand. And she noted at once that he wore a stunner, but neither she nor Yasa had been offered such a weapon.

They came out on the ramp, to stand for a moment just beyond the lock, looking about them at the wild desolation of this broken country. Her vision of a city—how could she have seen it here?

This earth was scored by deep crevices, blasted into a land which had repudiated life before they set foot on it. Ziantha's hands, without conscious willing, went to the bag she had fashioned, the cord of which hung about her neck, so that the lump rested against her breast. If she were to have any guide, that would be it.

Yasa moved up beside her.

"Singakok," the Salarika said softly. "Is *this* your city?"

She had good reason to question. In all that mass of tortured rock that lay about them there was no resemblance to anything wrought by the work of intelligent beings—unless the destruction itself could be taken for such evidence.

"I—I do not know!" Ziantha turned her head from side to side. Where was the tower, the great avenues—all the rest? Or had that vision been hallucination, born from some quirk of her own imagination and fed into her mind as a "seeing"?

"Which way do we cast?" Iuban, two of his men, armed and ready, caught up with them. "I do not see any signs of a city here. Are you playing games then?"

Yasa turned on him. "Know you nothing of the art of a sensitive, sky rover? The talent cannot be forced. It comes and goes, and sometimes not to any bidding. Let the girl alone; in her own time and way she shall pick our path."

There was little expression on his face, nor did his dead eyes show life. But Ziantha was aware of his emotions none the less, impatience and disbelief being well to the fore. And she did not think he would take kindly to any evasion he could detect. Also she was sure she was not clever enough to play the delaying role Yasa wanted. If she found any hint of what they sought she must use it to satisfy him.

It seemed that they were leaving the leadership of this expedition to her. And, with no way of escape, she walked slowly down the ramp, stepped out on the barren rock below. There she fumbled with the bag, unwrapped the lump, held it in her hands.

Ziantha closed her eyes. The answer came with the force of a blow which nearly beat her to the ground. There was the sensation that she stood in a city street amid a press of people, with the passing of strange machines. The force of life feelings, of random thoughts she could not understand, was so great it made her giddy.

"Ziantha!" A hand tightened on her arm. She opened her eyes. Yasa half supported her, the Salarika's eyes intent upon her.

"This—is—was a city," the girl answered.

Iuban had come to face them. "Well enough, but one we cannot search now—unless we can turn back time. Where do we go to look for anything that remains? Can you tell us that, dreamer?" He made a scoffing challenge of his demand.

There had been no selectivity to that impression of the city. Ziantha's hold on the artifact tightened. Suppose she were to open the crude outer casing, release the jewel inside, would that lead them to what they sought? But she shrank from that act. Let her try as long as she could to use it as it was.

"Let me try—" she said in a low voice, twisting loose from Yasa's hold. There was a ledge of rock nearby, and she reached that, to sit down, hunched over the lump. Wetting her lips, she forced herself to touch it to her forehead.

It was like being whirled through a vast flow of faces, voices. They shouted, they whispered, they grew large, dwindled, they spoke in tongues she had never heard, they laughed, wept, howled, screamed— She made herself try to steady upon one among the many, concentrate on learning what she could.

Singakok—Turan! The second name she held to, using it as an anchor that she might not be carried away in the sea of faces, deafened by the voices, the clamor of the long-vanished city.

"Turan!" she used the name to demand an answer.

The faces withdrew, formed two lines melting into one another, their cries stilled. Between the lines moved a shadow procession. That was Turan, and behind him was her place, her own place. She must follow—for there was no escape—

"What is she doing?" Very faint, that question.

"Be still! She seeks—" came in answer.

But that exchange had nothing to do with Turan. She must follow him. The shadows grew no denser, but they remained, a little ahead. No longer were there faces on either side—only Turan and her tie to him.

Now and then that scene shimmered, tore, as if it were fashioned of the thinnest gauze, shredded by a breeze. Then she saw only distorted rocks and a barren land that was not Singakok. When that happened she had to stop, call upon Turan, rebuild the vision.

Very dimly she heard chanting, sweet and high, like the caroling of birds released from captivity, or the thud of drums which were of the earth, the earth reluctant to lose Turan. Turan—

The shadows were gone, whipped away. Ziantha could not again summon them. She stood with the artifact before a great rise of bare red rock, a wall of cliff. But she knew that what she had sought lay behind it, that the artifact had led her to a place from which it had once come.

The girl looked back over her shoulder. Yasa, Iuban, his men, all were watching her.

"What you seek—" she said, the energy fast draining from her as it always did when she had made such an effort, "lies there." She pointed ahead at the rock, staggering then to an outcrop where she might sit, for she feared her trembling legs would no longer support her.

Yasa came to her quickly. "You are sure, cubling?"

"I am sure." Ziantha's voice was close to a whisper. She was so spent in her struggle to hold the vision that she longed only for rest and quiet, for no more urging to push her talent.

The Salarika held out two revive capsules, and Ziantha took them with a shaking hand, put them in her mouth to dissolve slowly. Iuban had gone to the face of the cliff, was examining it intently, and at a signal his men split to search left and right.

"I can see nothing—" he was beginning when the crewman to his right gave a hail. The Jack captain hurried toward him.

Yasa bent over Ziantha. "I told you—be slow—do not reveal anything before Ogan comes—"

"He is here, or near." Ziantha felt the aid of the revive. "In the early morning I had a message—"

"Ahhhh—" A purr of satisfaction. "It goes well, very well, then. And you play no game with Iuban; this *is* the place?"

Ziantha regarded the wall. "Turan lies there," she said flatly.

But who was Turan—or what? Why should this artifact bind her to him? She looked at the cliff, and now her fatigue was tinged with fear. Behind that—behind that lay— She wanted to scream, to run. But there was no escape, never any escape from Turan; she might have known that.

Only who was Turan? There seemed to be two identities within her now. One she knew; it was the Ziantha she had always been. But another was struggling for life—the one—the *thing* that knew Turan—Singakok—the one to whom she must never yield!

Iuban had been conferring with his crewmen, and one now headed back toward the ship while the Jack captain came to them.

"There are marks of a sealed way there. We shall have to laser our way in."

"With care," Yasa warned swiftly. "Or do you have a depth detect for such purposes?"

"With care, and a detect," he replied. Now he glanced past the Salarika to Ziantha. "What more can she tell us? Is this a tomb?"

"Turan lies there," the girl answered.

"And who is Turan?" he prodded her. "A king, an emperor, a stellar lord? Is this a Forerunner of a star empire, or only an ancient of some earthbound planet? What can you tell us?"

Yasa swept in between them fiercely. "She is tired—such reading weakens a sensitive. Get that storehouse open and let her psychometrize some artifact from within and she can tell you. But she must rest now."

"At least she brought us here," he conceded. And with that he tramped back to the walled-in door. But Yasa sat down beside Ziantha, putting her arm about the girl's shoulders, drawing her close, as she asked in a very low voice:

"Have you contact now with Ogan? It is now he must come."

Ogan? Summoning up what strength she had Ziantha formed a mind picture of the parapsychologist, sent forth mind-search. Harath had cut communication so summarily earlier she did not try him. The alien could be capricious on occasion, better aim directly for Ogan. Only she had no—

Answer? A flash of contact, as instantly gone. Ogan? It was not Harath, because even so light a touch would have revealed the alien. This had been wholly human. Ogan, then— but for some reason unwilling to accept a message. She said as much.

"Do not seek then. There may be a detect he has reason to fear. But as he did make contact, he will know where we are and the urgency of the matter. You have done well in this matter, cubling. Be sure I shall not forget what I owe you."

The crewman returned, another with him. Between them they carried a box and a portable laser—of the type used for asteroid mining. But it was the detect which Iuban first put into action.

Yasa and Ziantha joined him as he crouched over the box, studying the small visa-tape on its top.

"An open space, three cycles within," he reported. "The tomb chamber perhaps. Low frequency setting to bore us a door without any side flare."

He set the laser with care, aiming it twice at nearby rocks to mark the results before he tried it on the wall. Then he moved the finger of the beam up and down within the faint lines of the ancient opening, cutting out a space no wider than a man. The brilliant beam of a belt torch thrust into the space beyond.

"Let us go to Turan!" Iuban laughed.

Ziantha raised one hand to her throat, the other still cradled the artifact against her breast. She was choking, she could not breathe. For a second or so the sensation was so severe she felt that death itself was a single flicker of an eye-lid away. Then the sensation faded, and she could not fight as Yasa pushed her along hard on Iuban's heels through the break in the wall.

The Jack captain's lamp flooded the space into which they had come. But it showed dire destruction. This had been a tomb once, yes, and a richly furnished one. But other grave robbers had preceded them. There was a wreckage of plundered chests, now crumbling into dust, objects which had lost their meaning and value when they had been mis-handled by those in search of precious and portable loot.

"An abort!" Iuban swung the torch back and forth. "A thrice-damned abort!"

"Be careful!" Yasa cried and caught his arm as he would have moved forward. "We will not know that until after a careful, and I mean a very careful, search is made of what is still here. Tomb robbers often leave what seems of little value to them, but is worth much to others. So do not dis-turb anything—but widen the passage in that we may shift and hunt—"

"You think anything of value still lies in this muck?" But he did retreat a step or two. "Well, I think it is an abort. But if you can make something out of it—"

Ziantha leaned back against the wall. How could she fight this terrible fear that came upon her in waves, left her weak and sick? Did not the others feel it? They must! It penetrated all through this foul chamber, born not of the wreckage which filled three-quarters of it, but of something else—something beyond—

She turned and pushed through the crack of door, feeling as if that fear were reaching forth great black claws to drag her back. There was a shout behind, words she could not hear, for the beat of her own pounding heart seemed to deafen her. Then there were hands on her, holding her prisoner though she still struggled feebly to flee that place of black horror.

"Tried to run for it—" Iuban's voice over her head. But Yasa touched her, even as the iron grip of the captain held her.

"What is it?" demanded the Salarika. There was a note in her hissing voice which Ziantha had to obey.

"Death—beyond the far wall—death!" And then she screamed for the horror had her in its hold as if that formless evil rather than the captain kept her from flight, screamed and screamed again.

A slap across her face, hard enough to shock her. She whimpered in pain, at the fact that they would not understand, that they held her captive so close to—to— She would close her mind! She must close her mind!

And with the last bit of strength she could summon, Ziantha hurled the artifact from her desperately, as if in that act alone could she find any safety of body or mind.

"Ziantha!" Yasa's voice was a summons to attention, a demand.

The girl whimpered again, wanting to fall on the ground, to dig into the earth and stone as a cover, to hide—from what? She did not know now, only that it was terror incarnate, and it had almost swallowed her up.

"Ziantha—beyond the wall is what?"

"No—and no—and no!" She cried that into Yasa's face. They could not use her to destroy herself; she would not let them.

Perhaps Yasa could read her resolution, for she spoke now to Iuban. "Loose her! She is at the breaking point; any more will snap either her talent or her mind. Loose her to me!"

"What trick is she trying?" Iuban demanded.

"No trick, Captain. But there is something in there—we had better move with caution."

"Captain—look here!" One of the crewmen had knelt beside a rock to the right. He had picked up a shard in which was nested a glitter of spun silver. The artifact had broken open, the focus-gem must now be revealed. Iuban took that half of the figurine, pulled apart the protecting fiber. The gem blazed forth as if there were a fire lighted in it at this exposure to the open air. Ziantha heard the crewman give a low whistle. As Iuban was about to pick out the gem, Yasa spoke:

"Care with that. If it is what I think it may be, then much is now clear—"

"What it may be—" he echoed. "And what is that? An emperor's toy, perhaps?"

"A focus-stone," she replied. And Ziantha wondered at how Yasa had so quickly guessed.

"A stone," the Salarika continued, "used continually by some sensitive as a focus for power. Such things build up vast psychic energy over the years. If this is such a one and Ziantha can use it—why, no secret on this world pertaining to the race of the one who used it can be hidden from her. We may have found the key to more riches than a single plundered tomb!"

"And we may have listened to a likely tale," he countered. "I would see this proved."

"You shall. But not now; she is too spent. Let her rest while we make certain of what lies within here. And if this does prove an abort, we can try elsewhere with the stone."

Yasa would help her, Yasa *must* help her! Once they were alone she could explain, let the Salarika know that deadly peril waited any further dealings with Turan—or this world— or the focus-stone! If Ogan came, he would know the danger.

She could make him understand best of all that there were doors one must not open, for behind those lay— Ziantha would not let herself think of that! She must not!

The girl concentrated on holding that barrier within her so much that she was no longer entirely aware of what went on about her. Somehow she had got back to the ship, was lying on a bunk, shivering with reaction while Yasa gave her reassurance.

"Ogan—" Ziantha whispered. "Ogan must know—it is very dangerous."

Yasa nodded. "That I can believe. A stone of power—able to work through such a disguise. Perhaps only a linkage dares use it. Now rest, cubling, rest well. I shall keep these Jacks busy until Ogan comes and we are able to do as we would about the whole matter."

That Yasa had given her a sedating drug she knew and was thankful for. That would push her so deeply into sleep that dreams would not trouble her. And she carried with her that last reassurance. A linkage, yes—she, Ogan and Harath working together might be able to use the focus-stone. But not alone, she must not do it alone!

She was cold—so cold— She was lost in the dark. This was a dream—

"—another shot, Captain?"

"Try it. She's no use to us this way. And when that she-cat comes out of the one we used on her she'll be after us. Give it to this one now."

Pain and cold. Ziantha opened her eyes. There was a bright light showing broken things covered with dust, a wall beyond. She was held upright facing that wall in a grip she could not resist.

Iuban reached out, caught at her hair in a painful hold, for it was so short his nails scraped her scalp as his fingers tightened. So he held her to face him.

"Wake up, you witch!" He shook her head viciously. "Wake up!"

A dream—it must be a dream. This was Turan's place; they had no right here. The guards would come and then what would happen to them would be very painful, prolonged, while they cried aloud for the death which was not allowed them. To disturb the rest of Turan was to bring full vengeance.

"She's awake." Iuban, still holding her hair with that painful pull, looked straight into her eyes. "You will do this," he spoke slowly, spacing his words as if he feared she might not understand. "You will take this thing, and you will look into it and tell us what is hidden here. Do you understand?"

Ziantha could not find the words to answer him. This was a dream, it must be. If it was not— No, she could not! She could not use the stone where Turan lay! There was the gate to something—

"Ogan," cried her mind in rising terror. "Ogan, Harath!"

She met—Harath—and through him, with him, not Ogan— a new mind, one which greeted her search with a surge of power. Hold for us, it ordered.

"She has to handle the thing, I think," someone behind her said.

"Take it then!" Iuban set the weight of his will against hers.

She would not! But those behind her, those who held her upright here were forcing her arm up though she fought. Her strength was nothing compared to theirs.

"Harath—I cannot—they are making me use the stone! Harath—they make me—"

Iuban had caught one of her hands, was crushing her fingers, straightening them from the fist she tried to keep clenched. In his other hand she could see the blaze of the gem, afire with a life she knew was evil, though she tried to keep from looking at it.

77

"Harath!" desperately she pleaded.

"Hold—" came the answer. Harath's, together with that other's—the stranger's. "We are almost—"

Iuban ground the gem into the hollow of her palm. With his grip on her hair he pulled her head forward.

"Look!" he ordered.

His compulsion was such that she was forced to his will. The glowing stone was warm against her shrinking flesh. Its color deepened. It had life, power, reaching out, pulling her, drawing her through—

She screamed and heard shouting far off, the crackle of weapon fire. But it was too late. She was falling forward into the heart of the stone, which was now a lake of blazing energy ready to engulf her utterly.

7

The sickly sweetness of bruised camphor-lilies was drugging her; she could not breathe. No, she could not breathe because she was locked in here with Turan! Turan who was dead, as she would be when the air failed and she would enter the last sleep of all.

She was Vintra, war-captive from Turan's last battle, the one in which he had taken his deathblow.

Vintra? who was Vintra? Where was this dark place? Ziantha tried to move, heard a harsh clink of metal through the oppressive dark. She was—chained! Chained to a wall, and no frantic fight against those bonds left her with more than cut and bruised wrists and the knowledge that she had used up precious air by her struggles.

She was Vintra—no, Ziantha! Crouching against the wall she tried to sort out her whirling thoughts, decide which were true and which hallucinations. She must be caught in some trance nightmare. Ogan had warned her of such a danger. That was why she must never enter the deep trance alone. Nearby there must be one skilled enough to break the trance if she were caught in a killing hallucination.

Ogan—Harath— The thought of them steadied her.

In the tomb of Turan Iuban had forced her to focus on the gem. This was the result. But it was real! She felt the chains, gasped in the lack of air. She was—

Vintra! It was like the turning of a wheel in her head, making her first one person and then the other. Vintra was to die here, part of a funeral gift to Turan, because she was the only prisoner of note taken during the last skirmish at the mountain pass. In her a great rage surged against Turan and his kind. She would die here, gasping out her life like a korb drawn from its water home, but she would be avenged! And that avenging—

The pictures in her mind— What, who was she?

Ziantha! Once more the wheel had turned. She was Ziantha, and she must get back, out of the trance. Ogan— Harath—! Frantically the girl sent out mind-calls, begging for help to save her from this dream that was worse than any she had ever faced before on the out-plane, though it was true that when one was trained to enter a sensitive's calling one had to face all one's fears, meannesses of spirit. Ill acts were given form and substance in trances. Only when one conquered those did one win to psychic control. In the past such terrors had been real also, but now, as she forced herself to employ one familiar safeguard after another, there was no change. She had known this was different, that she had no defense here. No, she must be awakened, anchored to her own time and plane by more strength than she herself could summon.

Harath—Ogan! She made mind pictures, cast for them.

A faint stirring! Surely she had caught that! By all the power of That Which Was Beyond Reckoning, she had felt that answer! Ziantha turned all her talent force into one plea: draw me forth—draw me forth—or I die!

Yes! A stir—there was an answer. But it did not come straight, as she expected. It rather flowed, like water finding its way around great rocks half damming a river course, as if it fought.

"Harath! I am here! Come for me! Do not leave me to die in the dark, choking out life, imprisoned in what I cannot understand. Come!"

Not Harath!

There was a personality here. But not Harath—not Ogan. From the other plane then? She touched thought.

Shock, horror—a horror so great that that other personality was reeling as a man might under a deathblow.

"Help me," it cried. She could not understand. This had come at her call—why then—?

"Dead! Dead!"

An answer out of the dark fraught with terror.

"I am not dead!" Ziantha denied. She would not accept that, for if she did there would never be any escape. She would be caught in Vintra.

"Dead"—the repetition was fainter. Going—the other was going—to leave her here! No!

She might have screamed that aloud. The sound seemed to ring around and around in her head.

"No!"

There was silence through which she could hear the gasping from her laboring lungs. Then—from the other:

"Where is this place?"

Words—not mind-send, but words to hear.

"The tomb of Turan," she answered with the truth that Vintra knew.

"And I—I am Turan—" the voice grated. "But I am *not* Turan!" The denial followed the recognition swiftly, as if the same fear she had known when Vintra had taken over gripped him.

Sounds of movement. Then a mind command, quick and urgent: "Light!"

A glow, growing stronger. Why had she not thought of that? Straightway she sent her own energy to feed his, to strengthen the glow.

"There is no air, we shall die." She added her urgent warning.

"Go to the sunder plane, quickly!"

His command brought her mind back into the protective

pattern, which she should also have done for herself. She took the steps of out-of-body, something she had always been reluctant to try. And so, safe for a time, looked about her.

There lay the body from which she had just freed herself, tangled in chains. To her left was a two-step dais on which rested Turan, his High Commander's cloak spread over him, the lilies massed, brown-petaled, dying. Even as she saw him, candles at the head and foot of his resting place flared high.

"The spirit door!" that other's voice in her head. "There!"

She had not remembered, not until he spoke, for that was of Vintra's knowledge not her own. But there was the spirit door set in the rock above Turan.

"Draw back the bar there—"

Their only hope. For if that faintly twitching body she had just left died, then she was also lost. Ziantha made reentry, knew the life force was fast fading. With the last spurt of energy she could summon, she joined her power to the other's, fastened thought to the bar. Together they wrought; fear rose in her—they could not—

She heard a stir, for it was dark again, since all their talent was focused on that one act.

"My arm—my right arm—" wheezed the voice.

She fed him her power. And then she fell into darkness again without learning whether death came with it.

"Vintra!" Her body ached, she cried out with pain as hands pressed her ribs again and again, forcing air in and out.

"I live—let—be!"

There was light again. The candles flamed steadily to show the spirit door hanging open. From it came air, chill but blessedly fresh. Turan knelt beside her, now inspecting the fastenings of the chains.

"A pretty custom," he commented. "Human sacrifice to honor a war hero."

"You—Turan—" She tried to edge away from him. Turan was dead. Even now his body showed those wounds the priests of Vut had repaired that he might go to Nether World intact of person. Yet they looked fully healed, as if they had been ordinary hurts nature mended.

"Not Turan," he shook his head, "though I appear to share some identity with him from time to time. Not any more than you are Vintra. But it would seem we must play parts until we find a way back."

"You, you were the one with Harath!" Ziantha guessed. "The one who was coming when Iuban made me use the focus-stone."

"I was." But he did not identify himself further. "Now what is this about the focus-stone? Apparently some trick of psychometry hurled us back into this, and the more I know how and why the better. Tell me!" It was a sharp order, but she was only too willing to obey it.

He had found the trick of the chain fastening, and now they fell from her, and he kicked them away into a corner. Ziantha began her tale with the first sight of the artifact, and all that had happened to her since she had fallen under the peculiar spell that ugly lump with its hidden and perhaps fatal heart had exerted on her.

"A gem such as that now on your forehead?"

Startled, Ziantha raised her hands to her head. There was an elaborate headdress confining hair much longer than her own. And from those bands a drop set with a gem rested just above her eyes. She wrested the band from her so she could see the stone.

It was the focus-stone! Or enough like it to be. Ziantha thought she could tell with a touch, yet she dared not. Who knew what might happen if she tried again?

"Is it?" he who was now Turan demanded a second time.

Ziantha looked miserably at the crown. She had firmly exiled Vintra, but as she stared down at the stone that other identity stirred, gathered strength. Perhaps she might learn the power of the stone, but in doing so she could also lose that other who had been meant to die here in Turan's tomb.

"Vintra—Vintra might know—" she said with vast reluctance, but she could not suppress the truth.

"If the stone had power enough to hurl you into Vintra and me into Turan, then perhaps its results can be reversed. We must know. Look, you are not alone; my will backs yours. And I promise you I shall not let you be imprisoned in Vintra!"

He was Turan, the enemy, who could not be trusted (that was Vintra growing stronger, bolder). No—he was all the help she could have to win back to Ziantha and reality.

"I will try," she said simply, though she shrank from such exposure to whatever lay within the focus of this deadly bit of colored stone.

The ornament of the crown could be detached from the rest, Ziantha discovered. She unhooked the pendant, raised it to her forehead, and—

Turan's hands were on her shoulders; he was calling her, not in words, but in the powerful waves of mind-send.

"I was not able to learn—" she said in distress.

"Nornoch-Above-the-Waves, Nornoch of the Three Green Walls— The Lurla to be commanded—" He recited the strange names and words slowly, making almost a pattern of song.

"She who is D'Eyree of the Eyes—" Ziantha found herself answering, or adding. "Turan—what does that mean? I do not remember—I am saying words I do not understand."

She rubbed her hand wearily across her forehead. Her hair, loosened from the confinement of the crown, fell thickly about her shoulders like a smothering veil.

"You have returned to Vintra." He still kept that hold upon her, and his touch was comforting, for it seemed to anchor her to this body, controlled that feeling that she was about to whirl out and away from all ties with rational life.

84

"But before Vintra," he was continuing, "there was an-other—this D'Eyree, who had the talent, was trained in its use."

"Then I just 'saw' again—in a trance!"

"Yes. And this you have learned for us, though you may not presently remember. This focus-stone has its counterpart, which is tied to it by strong bonds, draws it ever, so that she using it is swept farther back in time. The one stone struggles to be united with the other, and that which lies in the past acts as an anchor."

"Vintra—"

"Vintra did not use the talent," Turan said. "To her the stone was only a beautiful gem, a possession of Turan's clan. But it is a thing unique in my knowing, an insensate thing which had been so worked upon as a focus that it has come to have a kind of half-life. Awakened, that half-life draws it, and those who focus upon it, so that it may be reunited with its twin. And unless that is done I believe that we are held to it."

"But if its origin lies beyond Vintra's time—how far beyond Vintra?" she interrupted herself to ask that, fearing the answer.

"I do not know—long, I think."

Ziantha clasped her hands tightly to keep them from shaking. The crown clanged to the floor.

"And if we can not find . . ." She was afraid to complete that question. If his fears were now as great as hers—she did not want to know. What were they going to do? If they could not return—

"At least," he said, "we shall not remain here. The spirit door is open. We'd best make what use of that we can."

He went to stand on the bier, looking up to the dark hole.

"You"—Ziantha moistened her lips and began again—"you —in *his* body—can you control it?"

To her knowledge, and through Ogan that was not too

85

limited, this experience was totally unknown. Of course the legends of necromancy—the raising of the dead to answer the questions and commands of those using the talent in a forbidden way—were known to more than one galactic race. But this type of transfer was new. Would it last? Could he continue to command a body from which life had ebbed before he entered it? She had come into Vintra while the other lived, merged in a way so that her stronger personality was able to push Vintra aside. But in his case—

He looked at her, the wavering candle flames making his face an unreal mask. "I do not know. For the present I can. This has not been done before, to my knowledge. But there is no reason to dwell on what might be; we must concern ourselves with what is, namely, that to linger here is of no use. Now—" He crouched below that opening and made a leap that she watched with horror, fearing that the body he called upon to make that effort would not obey. However, his hands caught the frame of the spirit door and held for a moment, and then he dropped back.

"We need something to climb on—a ladder." He looked around, but the grave offerings were all on the other side of the wall. There was nothing here but—

He was moving the bier end up. Then he caught up the chains, jerking them loose from the wall ring so he had a length of links.

"You will have to steady this for me," he told her briskly. One end of the bier was within the opening above. He draped the chain about his neck and climbed. Picking up the crown, careful not to touch the dangling gem, Ziantha came to his call, bracing and steadying the bier as best she could.

He was within the frame of the door, his head and shoulders out of her range of sight now. A moment later he was gone. The candles were burning low, but they gave light enough for her to see the chain end swinging through and knew that he must be fully out and prepared to aid her after him.

Moments later she shivered under the buffeting of a strong wind and the beginning of rain out in the open. Some of Vintra's memories helped her.

"The guards—" she caught at his arm. He was winding the chain about him like a belt, as if he might have further use for it.

"On a night like this," he answered, "perhaps we need not fear they are too alert."

It was wild weather. Her festive garment, for they had arrayed Vintra for this sacrifice in a scanty feast robe, was plastered to her body, and the wind whipped her long hair about her. The chill of wind and rain set her shuddering, and now she could see her companion only as a shadow in the night. But his hand, warm, reassuring, closed about her shoulder.

"To Singakok, I think." His voice, hard to hear through the wail of the wind, reached her with difficulty.

"But they will—" Vintra's fear emerged.

"If Turan returns, as a miracle of Vut's doing?" he asked. "The mere fact that I stand before them will give us the advantage for a space. And we need what Turan, or his people, know about that toy you carry. Guard it well, Ziantha, for it is all we have left to bring us back—if we can achieve a return."

Perhaps there was a flaw in his reasoning, but she was too spent by emotion, by what lay immediately behind her, to see it. Vintra shrank from a return to the place of her imprisonment, her condemnation to death. But she was not Vintra—she dared not be. And when he drew her after him, she yielded.

They came through a screen of trees that had kept the storm from beating them down. And now, from this height, they could see Singakok, or the lights of the city, spread before them.

"The guards or their commander will have a land car." Turan's attention was entirely on the road that angled toward the root of the cliff like a thin tongue thrust out to ring them round and pull them in for Singakok's swallowing.

"You can use Turan's memories?" Ziantha was more than a little surprised. Turan's body had been dead, emptied. How then could this other being know the ways of the guards?

"After a fashion. If we win through this foray we shall have some strange data to deliver. Yes, it appears that I can draw upon the memory of the dead to some degree. Now, try you Vintra also—"

"I hold her in check. If I loose her, can I then regain command?"

"That, too, we cannot know," he returned. "But we must not go too blindly. Try a little to see what you can learn of the city—its ways."

Ziantha loosed the control a fraction, was rewarded by memories, but perhaps not useful ones. For these were the memories of a prisoner, one who had been kept in tight security until she was brought forth to give the final touch to Turan's funeral.

"Vintra was not of Singakok—only a prisoner there."

"True. Well, if you learn anything that is useful, let me know quickly. Now, there is no use skulking here. The sooner we reach the city, the better."

They ended their blind descent of the heights with a skidding rush that landed them on their hands and knees in brush. If Turan found that his badly used body took this ill, he gave no sign, pulling her up to her feet and onto the surface of the road.

And they reached that just in time to be caught in the full, blinding glare of light from a vehicle advancing from the city. They froze, knowing that they must already have been

88

sighted. Then Turan turned deliberately to be full face to whomever was behind that light. They must see him, know him, if they would accept the evidence of their eyes.

Ziantha heard a shout, a demand to stand, rasped in the guttural tongue of the city. Men came into the path of the light, one wearing the weather coat of an officer, behind him two armsmen.

"Who are you?" The three halted warily, weapons at alert. They had hand disruptors, the officer an energy ray. Vintra's memory supplied the information.

"You see my face," Turan replied. "Name me."

"You have the seeming—but it must be a trick—" The officer stood his ground, though both the armsmen edged back a little.

Turan raised his hands to his throat, loosened and turned back the high collar of his tunic. The priests of Vut had closed his death wound, but it was still plain to see.

"No trick this. Do you mark it?"

"Whence came you this night?" The officer was shaken but he retained control. Ziantha granted him courage for this.

"Through that door which the Will of Vut leaves for every man to try," Turan answered promptly. "Now—I would go to Singakok where there is that I am called to do."

"To the Tower of Vut?"

"To the House of Turan," he corrected. "Where else would I go at this hour? There are those who await me there. But first, give me your weather coat."

Dazedly the officer loosed the fastenings and handed the garment over, though he made an effort not to touch Turan's hand in that process.

Shaking it out, Turan set it about Ziantha's shoulders. "This must do," he said, "until better serves you."

"That is an error," she thought-flashed to him. "In this

world we are enemies to the death! They will not accept such an act from you."

"To the death," he answered in the same fashion, "but not beyond. All things of this world are weighed now between us. If any ask, that I shall say." Then he spoke aloud:

"Two of us were left in that place, to abide the mercy of Vut; two return after his fair judgment. Of what happened it is not yet the time to speak."

One of the armsmen had put down his weapon, was peeling off his coat.

"Lord Commander, I was at Spetzk when you broke the rebel charge. Honor me by letting that which is mine be of service to you now." He came to Turan holding out the garment.

"This night I have done a greater thing, comrade. For your good will I give thanks. And now, I—we—must go to the House of Turan—by your aid."

Ziantha did not know what game he would play; she could only follow his lead. Within the curve of her arm, pressed tightly against her, was the crown with that pendant gem. To her mind they were pushing out into a swamp where at any moment some debatable footing would give way and plunge them both into disaster. But she allowed him to lead her to the car. And, silent, she took her seat in the passenger section, huddling within the weather coat for a warmth she could not find elsewhere. He settled beside her, and the vehicle turned to Singakok and all that might await them there.

8

"These," the message flashed to her, "do not have the talent, nor, it seems, any knowledge of it."

That her companion had dared to probe those with them made Ziantha anxious. It would seem that care was better than audacity now. Yet what he had learned made them free to use mind-touch.

"Can you then read their minds?" she asked in turn.

"Not to any extent—emotions rather. They have a different wave pattern. These are disturbed as would be entirely natural. The armsmen accept our appearance as a miracle of return, are in awe. The officer—" He checked, and when he did not continue, Ziantha prompted him:

"What of the officer?"

"I see someone, not clearly—someone to whom he feels he must report this as soon as he can. There is a shadow—" Again his thought trailed off.

Ziantha unleashed her own mind-seek, aimed now not at maintaining communication with her companion, but probing the emotions of those about her. Yes, she could understand Turan's bafflement. It was like trying to keep in steady focus a picture that blurred and changed whenever she strove to distinguish it in detail. But she recognized a woman. And that which was of Vintra awoke with a stormy memory.

Zuha M'Turan!

"The one to whom he would report," she relayed, "is the Lady of Turan. I think, Commander, that you—we—go now into a snarl of matters formerly a danger to him whose body you wear. It cannot be clearly read—but there is danger ahead."

"Which we knew from the first," he replied calmly. "So I am to beware, Lady? It would not be the first time that intrigue brought down a man, intrigue from those whose loyalty he had a right to expect was fully his. Now—we must try to delay any report. Can you bend his will, work upon it? I can sense something of his thoughts but not with the clarity I need for such influencing."

"I can try. But it is very difficult to keep in touch—this wavering—"

Ziantha centered her energy fully upon the problem. Though she knew well the theory of such suggestion, had worked it by Ogan's orders, she had done it surrounded by devices to monitor and restrain. To have used it anywhere outside those villa walls on Korwar would have alerted detects instantly. For such interference by a sensitive was so illegal that it would lead to brain-erase if one were caught practicing it. And the force so used was easily traced.

Delicately she probed, caught the picture of Zuha M'Turan. Drawing on Vintra's memory she built it firmly in her mind. And she felt her companion reach and touch that picture.

Bit by bit she achieved the effect she wanted to feed to the alien: that Zuha M'Turan already knew of this night's work, that it was part of a deep-laid plan not to be revealed yet, that chance had brought the officer into it, but that his superiors would be grateful in the future if he did nothing to disrupt it.

"Excellent!" Turan's accolade gave her confidence. "Now —feed it to him, and I shall back you."

As if she repeated a lesson learned by rote, Ziantha focused now on the mind of the man sitting on the other side of Turan, thrusting her image of Zuha and the message with all the vigor she could muster, feeling the backup force of the other. Twice she was certain she made clear contact, shared mind with the alien. Then, spent, after all this night had demanded of her, she could no longer fight.

Weariness swept in, a sea wave washing out all her strength of mind and will. As it ebbed she was left dull, uncaring, aware only of emptiness. Whether she had succeeded in what Turan had wanted of her she had no way of knowing.

They were into the streets of Singakok now. She was aware of lights through the curtain of rain, of people on the move. Vintra was pushing out of confinement within her; the old hates and fears which were a part of her double past surged up. And Ziantha was hard put to retain her own identity. Now she was Vintra, now Ziantha—and she was too tired to hold much longer.

The vehicle turned into a quieter side avenue where the buildings were farther apart, each separated by walls. This was the Way of the Lords—Turan's palace lay not too far ahead.

The ground car stopped at a gate; guards stepped out to flash a light into the shadowed interior. There was a gasp as that beam caught Turan.

"Admit us!" His voice was impatient as if the momentary halt had been an added irritation.

"Lord Commander—" the voice behind that beam of light was that of a badly shaken man.

"Am I to be kept waiting at my own door?" demanded Turan. "Open the gates!"

The guard jumped back, and the gate swung open. They drove between walls of dark vegetation, where rain-heavy foliage cut off any view beyond the borders. Then the car was through that tunnel and out before a sweep of steps leading to the imposing portal of the building.

Ziantha stumbled as she got out; her fatigue was such that those steps before her seemed insurmountable. But Turan

93

was at her side, his hand slipped under her arm, urging and supporting her. One of the armsmen hurried ahead to make a rattle of noise at the door.

That opened slowly just as they came to it. Light swept forth.

"Who comes to disturb the High Consort of the House of Turan? This is the day of third mourning—"

The man who began that indignant demand was now staring open-mouthed at Turan.

"Would you keep us out in this storm, Daxter? In my own door am I to be challenged?" Evidently Ziantha's companion would play his role boldly. Whether or not his boldness was a good defense, who could judge at the present moment?

The doorman retreated, staring. His face was visibly paler as he raised a hand, making a sign as if to ward off some supernatural danger.

"Lord Commander Turan!"

"Yes, Turan." He looked on into the hall. "The third day of mourning is over. Let the household be made aware of that."

"Lord Commander," Daxter retreated yet farther. "You—you are—"

"Dead? But, no, Daxter, I am not. Do dead men walk, talk, seek out their homes, their kin? And where is the High Consort? Let it be made known to her that there is no need for mourning."

"Yes. Lord Commander—"

"And see that this officer, these armsmen, be given the hospitality of the House. They have brought us through a wild night." He slipped off the weather coat and turned to the armsman to whom it belonged.

"Battle comrade, you named yourself; you now have the right to be comrade-in-arms with me. For I have come from a greater trial than any war, a fiercer battle than you can guess."

94

The man brought his hand up before his face, palm out, in salute. "Lord Commander, the honor of being ready to your service is mine. Be sure that when you call, I shall answer!"

To Ziantha the whole scene was like a tri-dee play, seen when one was half asleep and not too greatly interested in the story. If she could not relax soon, find some energy restorative, she would collapse.

"To my chambers now." Turan was giving more orders. "And you will bring food, wine. We have a long hunger and thirst, Daxter."

Ziantha knew they were climbing stairs, or rather, Turan was pulling her up step by step. But the rest was a haze until she was lying down and Turan was forcing between her lips a narrow spout from which came a hot, spicy liquid. Half choking, she swallowed again and again. It warmed her chilled body but also added to her lassitude. She could keep her eyes open no longer; her body was one long ache.

She was warm—too warm. Slowly she opened her eyes. Above her was a ceiling riotous in color, and, as her eyes focused, that color fitted itself within outlines of forms. But she had never seen those before. Those strange animals—if animals they were—or were they plants? This could not be her room in the villa. It was—

With effort she turned her head, looked across a wide bed. There were tall posts at each corner, and they provided support for what appeared to be living vines. Cream-colored flowers, touched with rose at petal tip, hung among those vines. And beyond the embowered bed was the wall of a room, its surface covered also with pictures that had the glint of inset metal here and there.

Ziantha pushed herself up with her hands to brace behind her. This strange room was *not* the villa. Where then was she, and how had she come here? Her thoughts were sluggish as she strove to remember the immediate past. Then, as if some barrier in her mind gave way suddenly, it all rushed in. Turan—Vintra—the tomb—their escape. This must be the palace in Singakok to which they had come. And Turan—where was Turan?

She looked about her wildly, needing at that moment the reassurance that she was not trapped here in the past alone. But there was no sign of any other in the chamber. More than a little lightheaded, the girl worked her way to the edge of the bed, slid her feet over to the floor, and tried to stand. The room seemed to dip and sway, and she had to hold on to the bed, creeping down to one of those leaf-covered posts and then hang on for support.

On the wall now facing her was a wide mirror and in that was the reflection of—not Ziantha—but Vintra! For a moment or two the shock of being confronted by a stranger was so great that she would not look, study, learn this new self. And then her need for control, for reasserting her will, dominated, and she made herself give that other a searching survey.

She saw a slender body hardly veiled by a transparent robe of pale rose to match the petal tips of the flower so near her cheek. No, it was more than slender, that body, it was gaunt. She was heavily browned on the arms to the shoulder, legs to the thigh, face and throat, the rest being a yellowish tint, as if some portions of her had been long exposed to sun and air. Her thick hair was in stringy wisps reaching well below her shoulders, not light, but a strange pale blue. And she believed that was natural, not some exotic tinting.

The eyes gazing back at her were bordered in lashes of a darker blue, just as the brows above them were, to her Ziantha memory, of that unnatural shade. For the rest, her face as well as her body were humanoid in contour, though both her forearms and lower legs had a very noticeable down or fluff of blue hair, much lighter against the brown skin.

So this was Vintra—Vintra of the rebels, Chieftainess of

the Foewomen of Kark, memory supplied that. But she must not allow that alien personality too much freedom. No, she must be Ziantha, or else there was no future for her.

The crown—the focus-stone! She looked about her. Where was that key, the only one which would—or could —open the way back? Her sharp anxiety gave her strength. She was able to loose her hold, move around the room in search. Table backed by another mirror, holding various small pots, a comb ready for service, two chests— She was struggling to lift the lid of the nearest when a sound brought her attention elsewhere.

One section of that painted wall had disappeared and in the opening stood another woman. Vintra's memory supplied a name.

Zuha M'Turan.

She held herself with the arrogant assurance of one who from birth had given orders that had never been questioned. But her face now, under its heavy mask of paint, silver overlay, was without expression, schooled to remoteness.

Her overrobe was as filmy as Ziantha's present covering and gave only an illusion of cloud over the inner and much shorter tunic. And her dark blue hair was piled into an elaborate coiffure held with pins from which fine wires supported small wide-winged insects of gauzelike filigree constantly in motion. About her waist was a belt from which depended small chiming bells and more encircled the tops of those tight-fitting silver boots showing through the folds of her upper robe.

She did not speak as she crossed the threshold. Behind her the door slipped shut; they were alone.

Ziantha was wary. Though she had not tried mind-seek, she could sense that danger had entered with the High Consort. Where was Turan? Had that body failed her companion? Would he now be returned to the tomb, she with him? But she was not Vintra to be easily handled—she had a defense

97

and weapon in her own mind that she would use to the utmost.

She must learn what had happened to Turan. Delicately, as she might have made the first attempt to pierce the structure of an explosive that could blast off in her face, she used mind-seek.

The alien wave pattern defeated any open reading. But that this woman hated her, and that there was fear with that hatred, yes, that could be read. Turan—Ziantha tried to bring some feeling for him to Zuha's mind.

The thought of Turan brought an explosion—seething hatred! With it, a fear near panic. Zuha had both. What she felt for Vintra was as nothing compared to the emotions which ravaged her now, although her outer facade gave no sign of that storm within.

But Ziantha had gained a little. Turan was alive—and this woman feared that. She had wanted, had believed, her consort dead—and he lived. Not only lived, but she believed him now an ever-present threat whom she must find a way to finish.

"Sorceress!" Zuha flung that single word as she might have used a flamer to char Ziantha. "You will not gain from this shadow-trickery you have wrought! Be sure that I will see to that!"

"I have wrought no trickery. There was the choice of Vut, the door given every man. If by Vut's will one comes through it, back to life, how can the right or will of that be questioned?" Vintra's knowledge, to draw upon at her time of need. Ancient beliefs these, long given only lip service by the sophisticated nobles.

Vut's priests taught of possible body resurrection through the spirit door, which could only be opened from within the sealed tomb. Fabled miracles, legendary accounts of such returns kept Vut as a power. His priests now would sustain

Turan in his return for the very reason that his appearance was a bolster to belief.

"Turan is dead. What outland sorcery do you use to make him move and follow your will? You shall tell me and he shall—"

But before the fury which burned her totally overcame all caution, Zuha was silent. It was plain that she refused to accept any thought of a miracle. Perhaps her questions might bring about discovery. Though the alien had no vestige of talent, Ziantha was certain of that—unless it existed on another range of mind-wave entirely.

"Turan is not dead. Have you not the evidence of your own eyes?" She must tread very warily. Zuha, the girl believed, was near to that pitch of mingled fear and rage that might lead to some hasty attack.

"The evidence of my eyes, say you? Yes, and the evidence of the mouthing priests also. Whether they think sorcery or not, they will not say it, lest Vut lose the advantage of this. But Turan was dead, now he lives—or his body walks—" Her hand moved in that same design the armsman had used. "This is not Turan." This last sentence was delivered with an emphasis that made it a declaration of war.

"And if it is not Turan," the girl countered, "who then is he?"

"Rather *what* is he, sorceress? What have you called from the Cold Depths to bring you out of Turan's tomb? Be sure that we shall learn, and in that learning you will have no profit. The death with Turan shall be as nothing compared to the end your dabbling in shadow lore will bring upon you."

"So it is sorcery, my High One, my First Companion, which brings me back to you?"

Ziantha had been so intent upon their confrontation, as apparently had Zuha, that his entrance had gone unmarked. For it was Turan who stood there, his gaunt face seamed with the wound of his last battle. In this full light he was no pleasant sight, for his skin was a pallid gray, and only his eyes were alive. That this body still served its inmate was a wonder to Ziantha.

"You speak of sorcery," he moved closer when Zuha did not answer, "but you do not speak of the infinite mercy of Vut, not even when your many prayers to him for my well-being have been so mightily answered. Why this change in you, my dear companion, my High Consort? Have you not told me many times that my death would mean your death also—that you would revive the ancient and highest custom of our people and joyfully follow me through the dark way if Vut chose that I should walk first? But who shared my tomb? Not you, for all those loving vows. Rather did you send with me one who was my battle enemy, who would carry with her no love to ease my path, only hate to draw upon me the shadow wraiths and evils. So did your promises come to little in the final hour of farewell. Is that not so, Zuha of the sweet tongue—of the many lies?"

As he advanced, she shrank back from him. And now under that masking of overlay her mouth worked; her features showed emotion at last. A portion of her mask loosened and fell from her skin as her lips twisted and tightened as if to hold within her some shriek of fear. Back she went before his slow steady talk.

"No! Do not come nigh me, dead man! Back! Get you back to the Cold Depths, from which you crawled, from which that sorceress drew you!"

"From the Cold Depths? Was that what you wished upon me, Zuha? Ill wishing, was it not? Perhaps it was your underdealing that brought me back; perhaps Vut would not be mocked by empty words and so gave me life to serve his purpose. That would be fitting—"

Her back was against the wall now. She flung out her other hand, felt along that surface. Then the hidden door opened and she fell rather than moved through it, scrambling back and away as it closed again, leaving Ziantha and him together.

"Guilt gives birth to fear," he commented, as if to himself. "How deep her hatred must lie. I wonder in what it is rooted."

"Turan"—Ziantha demanded his attention—"what have you learned?"

"A little in the time they left me free. It has taken much contriving on my part to keep out of the priests' hands. They would have me among them for examination, since a miracle is so much to their advantage. So far I have held them off. And I have discovered that, in spite of the intrigues within this palace, Turan also has some faithful followers. It was from one of those that I gained what knowledge I have of this." He put his hand within the breast of his tunic and brought out the focus-stone.

"Before the outbreak of the rebellion, Turan made a voyage in the southern sea with the fishers of the giant croobcrabs. There a tumult of nature struck without warning, hitting the fleet, no natural storm. From the description I was given it might have been the result of an underseas eruption, followed by a tidal wave. At any rate they found themselves luckily still afloat thereafter—but only just, for the power of their ship was far reduced. The ocean was much roiled, and dead things from the depths floated on the surface.

"Soon after, they sighted land where no land existed on their charts—an outcropping of rock encrusted with marine life, showing it had until lately been long underwater. At Turan's urging the captain sent a small boat ashore on this new-risen coast, and they made two finds. One where there had been a raw break in a ledge disclosing therein a piece of wall not formed by nature.

"Turan would have had them labor to uncover more, but

there came two aftershocks which shook the island. And the captain feared for the ship and wanted to be out of such dangerous proximity to a land mass they thought might sink again. They were on their way back to their ship's boat in some haste when Turan became separated from the rest.

"He did not join them at once, and the captain at last shouted to him to come or else be left behind. When he arrived he did not say what had detained him, only his clothing bore marks as if he had been lifting rocks covered with sea slime. And he said he had sighted what appeared to be an inscribed rock. But it was plain he was highly excited, and he tried to bring pressure on the captain to anchor nearby, to send in another party in the morning. However there was the threat of a storm, and the captain would not agree.

"Storm came rightly enough, driving them far off course, exhausting their power unit so that they had to put into one of the small ports as soon as possible. And though Turan talked now and again of returning to this risen land, the rebellion broke shortly after his return."

"What relation has this to the focus-stone?" Ziantha asked.

"These people do not use sensitives as we know them. But they have certain girls kept in the House of Vut who can go into trances and then answer questions the priests set to them. Apparently their talent is very limited and quickly exhausted, rendering each girl incapable after one or two sessions. Thus the power is the monopoly of the priests, well guarded, used only in times of stress.

"Turan exerted his influence with a priest of the Third Rank who had access to these girls. He produced this gem and asked for its history. Whatever the priest told him was unsettling, for he straightway had it set (he had hitherto carried it on his person) into the crown made for the High Consort to wear to her future entombing. There it remained until Zuha ordered it set on your head when she would have

you play the role set for her during her many earlier protesta-
tions of loyalty and love for her husband."

"And this follower of Turan told you all this? Did he not
suspect when you questioned him concerning a matter you
should have already known well?"

Turan's set lips moved in a counterfeit of a smile so
ghastly Ziantha looked away in a hurry.

"I saw that he recognized the stone and was astounded to
see me handling it. The rest I picked from his memory bit
by bit, only he did not know that. In this world a sensitive
has that advantage. But that this was found on that island,
I believe. Only whether that island still exists—that is another matter. And if the twin stone lies anywhere, that island
would be the first place to look."

"If you have any charts as a guide we might make sure."
Ziantha remembered her success with the star charts.

"Those are what I—we—must locate and speedily. As I
say, I cannot much longer spar with the priests and keep
out of their Tower of Vut. And even if their sensitives are
of the lowest grade they might discover the Turan who returned is not what they believe. Then Zuha could well raise
the cry of sorcery against us both and gain her wish to see
the last of her Lord Commander forever. We have very little
time—"

She looked at him and nodded. Vintra's body served her
well, and to look in the mirror reassured her that she was
alive. But, Turan, with those deep-closed wounds, that gray
face—he was suspect, and she marveled he had managed so
well this long.

9

The need for haste was so great it was as if someone trotted on their heels, urging them in whispers to run—run. She had found an undertunic, such as Zuha wore, in one of the chests and bundled over it a longer, semitransparent robe. She now caught that up in both hands to free her feet as they sped along a corridor that Turan said linked the women's quarters with his own.

Though once or twice they heard the sound of conversation or movement in rooms they passed, no one came into the hall. And, as far as mind-touch reported, they passed unseen. She could hardly believe fortune was favoring them so much.

If any record of Turan's voyage existed, that might be found among his private accounts. But to seek blindly was to waste their precious time. It would require both their talents, one to keep sentry, the other to sift out knowledge, as she had in Jucundus's apartment.

It was difficult to remember now that she was not only on an alien world, but in a time so far lost to her own that this city, these people were not even legends. Ziantha felt no wonder, only the driving need to escape, to find again her own place, dangerous though it might be. For those dangers were familiar, and now they seemed, by comparison, not to be perils at all, but a well-settled pattern of life. It is the unknown that always carries with it the darkest fears.

"Here—" Turan was at a door, waved her to him.

"Records?" She looked around her for something familiar.

Even if it might be the very ancient scrolls of actual writing she had seen in a museum.

"For secrecy perhaps, or even because of custom they were kept thus."

He had gone to a cabinet and now brought forth bunches of short cords, knotted together at one end, the rest flapping free. Along each of these many lengths were spaced beads of different shapes and colors. Ziantha stared. To her these made no sense. Records—kept by beads knotted at irregular intervals on bits of cord? That was a device she had never heard of. She looked to Turan, unable to believe that he meant what he said.

As he ran his fingers along the cords, he paused to touch a bead here and there.

"A memorization device. In our own time this would be used by a very primitive tribe that had not yet mastered the art of writing in symbols. Yet it can be a personal code, locked for all time. Apparently very secret records are kept here in this fashion. Each type of bead, each knotting, whether it be a finger width less or more from the next, has a meaning. The keeper of such can sit in the dark and 'read' these by running them through his fingers."

"If they are Turan's, then you should be able—"

He shook his head wearily. "I have only very fleeting touch with Turan's memories, and those grow less and less. I—I dare not use too much of my power; it is needed to control this body."

So he was admitting that he was having trouble with the Turan shell? Ziantha put out a hand, stirred the mass of cords. If they were in code, a code known only to him who had devised them, it would require intense concentration to gain anything from them.

Compared to this, dealing with the sealed tapes in Korwar was play for a beginner. For the tapes had been clearly inscribed by one of her own species. An alien code, devised by an alien— Well, since this key was the only one offered them she must try.

"You hold watch then?"

At his nod, she took up the nearest assortment of cords. They were silken soft, and the beads glinted blue, white, and vivid orange-scarlet. She slipped the packet back and forth through her fingers.

Emotion—hate—a vicious and deadly hate, as sharp and imperiling in its intent to threaten her reading as if the cords had taken on serpentine life and struck at her. With a little cry, she threw the bunch from her.

"What is it?"

Ziantha did not answer. Instead she held her hand palm down over the whole collection. Not quite touching, but in her mind seeking what source had broadcast that blast that had met her first probe.

"These—these have been recently handled, by some one who was so filled with hate and anger that emotion blankets all. Unless I can break that I can do nothing."

He lowered himself wearily onto a bench, leaned his head back against the wall, his eyes closed. And without the life of his eyes—Ziantha shuddered, would not look at him. It was as if a dead man rested there. How long could he continue to hold Turan in this pseudo-life?

"Who is responsible? Can you learn that?"

She took up again the first collection. Strong emotion could fog any reception of impressions, and she was already handicapped by trying to read alien minds. She wadded the beads and cords into a packet, held that to her forehead, trying to blot out all else but the picture she must have.

Zuha—yes, there was no mistaking the High Consort. But there was another influence. The girl tried for a name, some identification which perhaps Turan could recognize in turn. Zuha's hate, her frustration—those were so strong a wave that they were as blows against her, yet she probed.

"Zuha," she reported. "But there is another, some one behind Zuha. They came here seeking knowledge they did not discover. Zuha was very angry; she needed something she wanted desperately to find here. She—I think that she took some of these with her—the ones she believed important."

"If we can find no chart soon . . ." His thought trailed away.

Time—she could not defeat time. Ziantha tossed the cord bundle back with the others. Had she hours, perhaps days, she could sort through these. There must be another way, for she did not have those hours or days. She need only glance at Turan to know that.

An island risen from the sea, and on it somewhere a twin to the stone, an equal focus piece. Their piece tied to it, and they, apparently, tied to the first. If they could not release those ties, Turan would die again, and so would she—at the hands of Zuha—and no pleasant death.

One could believe that some essence of personality survived the ending of the body. Those with the talent were sure of that. But inbred in their varied species was so firm a barrier against their body's dismissal that they could not face what man called "death" without that safety device of struggle for existence taking over control. She would not accept the fact that she, Ziantha, was going to come to an end in this world which was not hers, any more than she believed that her companion could likewise surrender.

An island from the sea, and a stone found there— The girl strode back and forth, thinking furiously, before the bench on which Turan had half collapsed. There was one way, but she could not do it here. Not in the midst of enemies when at any moment those who had no reason to wish either of them life could come in upon them. But where?

Ziantha paused, looked around, tried to be objective. She had Vintra's memories to call upon and she did that recklessly. These people had aircraft. There was a landing port outside the city where such were kept. If Turan could pilot one—if they could first reach that landing port—commandeer one of the craft— Too many ifs, too many things that might stand between. But it was her—perhaps their—only hope.

She dropped down beside Turan, took his cold hand to hold between her two warmer ones, willing strength back into him. He opened his eyes, turned his head toward her.

Again that ghastly smile came. "I endure," he said, as if he not only meant to reassure her, but himself. "You have thought of something—what? I would think clearer but I must hold on, and at times that takes all my power."

"I know. Yes, I have thought of something. It may be far beyond what can be done, but it is all I have to offer. When I go into deep trance I must be in a safe place—"

His eyes were very intent. "You would try that, knowing what may come of it?"

"I can see no other way." She wanted him with desperate longing to deny that, to say there was another way, that she need not risk again the baleful influence of the stone that had already cost them so much. But he did not. Though he still regarded her closely, his mind-shield was up, and she believed he was testing her plan for feasibility.

"It is a way—" he said slowly. "But you are right, we must have privacy and safety before you try it. I do not believe we shall find either here. Turan's memories are so little open to me that I do not know what intrigues may be in progress. But they threaten from his own household. It is certainly not the first time a noble family came to an end by being torn apart from within. And where shall we find safety? Have you a plan for that also?"

"A weak one." She again wanted him to refuse, to prove her wrong. "These people have air transport. If we could get one—they are not too unlike our own flitters, I think—we might reach the sea. Find some safe place on the shore to give me time for deep trance—"

"It seems—" he was beginning when Ziantha whirled to face one of the mural-concealed doors in the wall.

The noise, a faint scratching, made her look about for

something to use as a weapon. She was reaching for a tall vase on a nearby table when Turan pulled himself from the bench, walked with a slow, heavy tread to release the portal.

A man squeezed through a crack hardly wide enough to admit his stocky body and shut that opening at once behind him. The hair on his head was streaked with light patches, and his face was seamed with two noticeable scars.

"Lord Commander, thank Vut you are here!" He looked beyond Turan to Ziantha. "Also the outland witch with you."

"There is trouble, Wamage?"

The man nodded vigorously. "More than trouble, Lord Commander; there may be black disaster. She"—into that single pronoun he put such a hiss that he spat the word in anger and disgust—"she has sent to the priests. They are to take you and"—he pointed with his thumb to Ziantha—"this one to the Tower of Vut, that the miracle may be made manifest to all on the Tenth Feast Day. But they do not intend that you shall ever reach sanctuary. Behind all is Puvult, Lord Commander! Yes, you exiled him half a year gone, but there have been rumors he returned while you hunted the rebels northward. Since—since you were tomb-laid, he is seen openly. And secretly within these very walls!"

"The High Consort then welcomed him?" Turan asked.

"Lord Commander, it has long been said that she favors the younger branch of your House over the elder." Wamage did not quite meet Turan's eyes. It was as if he had news to give, but feared to offend.

"And with me tomb-laid then Puvult comes into headship?" If Turan meant that for a question, it did not alert Wamage, as far as Ziantha could tell, into any suspicion of his lord's memory.

"You spoke that with the truth-tongue, Lord Commander. They thought you gone—then you return—"

"With the added power of a miracle," Turan commented. "I can see how they want now to finish me."

Wamage ran his tongue over his lips. Once more he would

not look at Turan but kept his eyes at some point over the other's shoulder.

"Lord Commander," he paused as if seeking courage to continue, and then went on in a rush of words, "*she* says that you are still tomb-laid—that this—this witch Vintra has only made a semblance of a man. Though one may touch you, as I have done, and you are firm and real! But *she* says that if you are taken to Vut the force will depart, and all men will see that this is sorcery and no real return. The priests, they are angry. For they say that in the past, Vut has returned men to life when their purposes here are not fully accomplished. And they do not believe her but want all the people to witness Vut's power. So they will come for you—only *she* has a way to make sure you do not reach Vut."

Turan smiled. "It would seem that she does not really believe in her own argument that I am but a rather solid shadow walking, or she would leave it to Vut to answer the matter."

Wamage made a small gesture. "Lord Commander, I think she believes two ways—she is fearful her own thought may be wrong. If you die again—then Vut's will is manifest."

"But I do not intend to die again." Turan's voice was firm. It was as if his strong will fed the talent which kept him alive. "At least not yet. Therefore I think I shall be safer—"

"We can get you to the Tower, Lord Commander. Vut's priests will then make a defense wall of their own bodies if the need arises!" Wamage interrupted eagerly.

Turan shook his head. "Do my own armsmen of Turan-la"—a shade of confusion crossed his face. "My armsmen of Turan-la," he repeated with a kind of wonder, Ziantha thought, as if he heard those words but did not fully understand them. Ziantha feared his confusion was visible to Wamage. But it would seem that the other was so intent upon his own message of gloom that his thoughts were for that alone. For he burst out then hotly:

"*She* sent them north after—after your entombing, Lord Commander. They were battle comrades of yours; they knew how you felt concerning Puvult. Me you can command under this roof, and Fomi Tarah, and of the younger men, Kar Su Pyt, Jhantan Su Ixto, and we each had armsmen sworn to us, as you know. Enough, Lord Commander, to see you safely to the Tower."

Turan was frowning. "There is another, not of this household, so he might not be suspected or watched. He lent me his weather coat on the night I returned—"

"Yes. I have sought him out. His father is a Vut priest, one Ganthel Su Rwelt. They live on the southern coast—the boy came with the levy from Sxark a year ago."

"From the southern coast!" Turan caught the significance of that at once. "Can you get word to him secretly?"

"I can summon him, but, Lord Commander, as you well know there are eyes and ears awake, watching, listening always amid these walls."

Turan sighed. His gaunt face looked even less fleshy, as if his grayed skin clung tighter and tighter to his skull.

"Wamage." He returned slowly to his bench, sat down as if he could no longer trust the effort standing erect caused him. "I would leave this palace, the Lady Vintra with me. But I do not wish to go—as yet—to Vut. There is something to be done, something of which I learned of late, which cannot be left while I tend this ailing body of mine. For time may be fatal. I must be free to move without question or interference. Now I call upon you for your aid in my service, for if battle comrades cannot ask this, then what justice lies in this world?"

"Truth spoken, Lord Commander. Can you depend upon no other for this deed which must be done?" There was a furrow of what Ziantha believed to be honest anxiety between Wamage's bushy brows. If Turan had not managed to gain the loyalty of his High Consort, in this man, at least, he had one faithful follower.

"No other. I have spoken truth to you; now I shall add

more. You know of my visit to the land that the sea gave up? Only recently you spoke of this—"

"A place you have often mentioned yourself, Lord Commander. You wished to take a ship of your own and go seeking it again, but the rebels broke out. But—what of it?"

"Just this—there I made a great find, a find which I must now uncover for my own safety."

"Lord Commander, you are in some fever dream, or else"—he swung to Ziantha, his face hard with suspicion—"there is some truth in the High Consort's babble, and this rebel wanton has bewitched you. What could lie on a rock in the sea that would aid you now?"

"Something very old and very powerful, and this is no bewitchment. For what lies there I saw long before Vintra came into my life."

"The gem! The gem which you took to Vut's tower and thereafter put from you, having it made into tombwear so that none could lay hand on it."

"In part, yes, but only in part. How think you that the Lady Vintra, wearing it in a tomb crown, was moved to come to my aid, brought me again to this very room? There were ancients of ancients. Do not men declare that they had strange knowledge we do not possess? What of the old tales?"

"But those are for children, or the simple of mind. And we do with the aid of machines made by our own hands what they did in those tales. Who could fly save with a double-wing?"

"They, perhaps. There were things of great power on that island, Wamage, how great I did not even guess then. I thought of such treasure as delights the eye; now I know it was treasure for the mind. With what I once found there and what still awaits to be discovered, I shall be armed against the forces ready to pull me down. Has part not already brought me from the tomb?"

"And how do you reach the island?"

"By your aid and that of this youth from Sxark. You shall

arrange for me and this lady—for she has learned part of the secret—"

Wamage moved with a speed Ziantha had not expected. Only the flash of mind-reading alerted her. He would have flamed her down with a small beamer he brought from his sleeve, but she had thrown herself flat.

"Wamage!" Turan was on his feet. "What do you do?"

"She is Vintra, Lord Commander. Every rebel drinks lorca-toast to her at night. If she has such command over any part of your fate she is better dead!"

"And me with her, is that what you would want, Wamage? For I tell you, it is by her I live, and without her further aid I cannot continue to do so."

"Sorcery, Lord Commander. Have in the priests and gain their aid—"

From where she crouched, Ziantha put all her talent into a mighty effort. His voice suddenly faltered, his hand dropped limply to his side, and from his fingers the beamer thudded to the carpeted floor. She retrieved it swiftly. The operation of it she saw was simple. One aimed and pressed a button. What the results would be Vintra's memory supplied; they were both spectacular and fatal.

"You should not have told him," she mind-sent.

"We need him. Otherwise we can make one blunder after another and achieve nothing."

To Ziantha's thinking one blunder had already been made, but she would have to accept Turan's plan. Could it be that he was making such an effort to retain control of his body that he no longer reasoned clearly, and the time would come when she must take command?

Reluctantly she released Wamage from the mind-lock. The man shook his head as if to banish some feeling of dizziness. As full consciousness returned to him Ziantha laid the beamer on the bench at Turan's hand.

"Look you, man of Singakok." She had from Vintra the heavily accented voice of the rebel leader. "I have now no weapon. There lies yours. At whose hand does it lie? Do you think that if I were your enemy in this hour I would disarm myself before you and your lord? I have no love for Singakok. But that which was beyond any struggle of ours faced me in the tomb of Turan, and he and I were bound together in this. Take up your weapon if you do not believe me, use it—"

If he tries that, Ziantha thought—if I have gambled too high—I hope Turan can stop him. But Wamage, though he put out his hand as if to carry out her suggestion, did not complete that move.

"She speaks the truth," Turan said. "She stands unarmed in the midst of her enemies, and she speaks the truth."

Wamage shook his head. "She is one of tricks, Lord Commander, as you know. How else have the rebels held us off this long? It is their tricks—"

"No trick in this. Vintra is no longer of the rebels."

"Do you want an oath on that before the altars of Vut?" Ziantha demanded. "I was bound to another cause by those hours in the dark before the spirit door opened. Do you think any man or woman could pass through such an ordeal as that and not come forth unchanged? For the present I am pledged to the Lord Commander and will be so until his mission is accomplished." She hoped that Wamage believed her—for in this she spoke Ziantha's truth.

Wamage looked from one to the other. "Lord Commander, I have been a battle comrade of yours since the action at Llymur Bay. I am sworn by my own choice to your service. What you wish—that shall it be."

Was this surrender coming too easily? Ziantha tried mental probe. The confusing in and out pattern of the alien mind could deceive her, whereas with her own kind she could easily have assessed friend or enemy.

"What I wish is a double-wing and the armsman from Sxark as a guide. The hour is late, and I must move tonight."

"It will be difficult—"

"I have not said this would move with ease; it is enough

that it does move!" Turan's voice took on a deeper note; there was authority in the look he turned upon the other. "For if we do not go at once, we may be too late."

"That is also true," Wamage agreed. "Well enough." He became brisk, producing weather coats from one of the coffers, these with head hoods, and, as he pointed out, no insignia.

Part of the way out of the palace they could follow corridors private to the Lord Commander, where none could intrude without invitation—A fortunate custom, Turan noted to Ziantha as Wamage went ahead to make sure of their clear passage in the public parts of the building.

"Do you trust him?" Ziantha did not. "He may be more loyal to what he considers best for you than to any order from you. Vintra is too long and bitter an enemy for him to accept otherwise."

"We can not lean too heavily on trust, no. But can you see any other way to get us out of this trap? If he is loyal we have won; if he plays a double game, we shall have mind-search to warn us. It is a pity we can not read their patterns better."

But it seemed Wamage would prove loyal. He led them through an inconspicuous side entrance to a waiting car.

"The armsman will meet us at the port, Lord Commander. But we have half the city to cross. And much can happen before we get there."

"So let us be on our way!"

Wamage slipped behind the controls of the vehicle. It was smaller than the one which had brought them there, and Ziantha was cramped tightly in beside Turan. Wamage was immediately in front of her, and she must be instantly alert, she knew, to any sign that he was not carrying out his orders. Half the city to cross—it would be a long time to hold that guard. Turan had raised barriers again, perhaps because he had to retain his talent to aid his own feat of endurance.

10

Under other conditions, Ziantha thought fleetingly, she would have watched about her with wondering eyes. She was doing what no other, not even the Zacathans with all their learning, had been able to accomplish, seeing a Forerunner civilization. But all that concerned her now was her own escape from it. It was necessary to concentrate on Wamage throughout this journey.

It would seem he was faithful to Turan's trust. At least the car traveled steadily, without hindrance, first along quiet streets and then along those filled with heavier traffic. If their escape had been discovered they were not yet pursued.

Wamage wove a twisted way from broad avenue to cross street and back. Ziantha had never had too keen a sense of direction; for all she knew they could be heading directly away from their goal. And Vintra's memory held little of Singakok.

The lights were bright as they took a last turn coming to a place where many cars were parked. Wamage slowed as he transversed this line of waiting vehicles, heading on past a lighted building.

To one side was a vast expanse lighted in part by rows of set flood lamps. There Ziantha saw one of the aircraft come into the light, turn rather clumsily, and rush forward, lifting after its run into the air. It was unlike the flitters of her own world, having fixed wings and apparently needing the for-

116

ward run to make it airborne, rather than rising straight up as was normal.

Yet the Vintra part of her cringed at the sight of it, projecting to Ziantha a vivid and horrifying memory of death falling in objects that exploded upon impact. Objects that came from such a machine.

Was Turan a pilot? Vintra had no such knowledge. As Ziantha probed she received the impression that such a skill was difficult to learn and required long tutorage. Or was Wamage to serve them so, accompany them on what might be a vain search? Did Turan plan to take the other fully into his confidence? Or did he propose to put a mind-lock on the alien and so bend him to their aid? That she did not believe could be held for any length of time.

Wamage drove on. The lights were fewer. They now passed a line of flyers. He circled at the end of this and stopped by one much smaller craft.

What might have been a torch flashed in the night. Wamage turned off the lights of the ground car and leaned out of the window to call softly:

"Doramus Su Ganthel?"

"To answer, Commander!" came swift answer.

"You have done well." Turan spoke for the first time since they had left the palace. "My thanks to you, battle comrade."

"It is in my mind that perhaps I have done ill," Wamage replied, a tired, heavy note in his voice. "I do not know why you must do this thing—" He had half hitched about in his seat. "Lord Commander, this woman is your deadliest enemy. She is Vintra who swore before the Host of Bengaril to have your head on the tri-pole of rebel victory. Yet now—"

"Now, by the will of Vut, she serves me as no other can. Think you where I have just come from, Wamage. If she wanted me dead would I not have remained there?"

"The High Consort speaks of sorcery—"

"For her own ends, and that you also know, Wamage. Was

it not you who warned me of her, not once, but twice and more? I tell you that when I return all which puzzles you now will be resolved. But if I do not go—then between the High Consort and the priests I will indeed be returned to whence I came and that with haste."

Wamage sighed so heavily Ziantha could hear him. "That I cannot doubt, Lord Commander, having heard what I have heard. But if there is a third choice—"

"For my safety, Wamage, in this hour there is not! And above all what I must do now must be speedily done. The longer I waste here—the more chances there are for failure—"

He stepped out of the vehicle, and Ziantha made speed to follow him. The waiting armsman came to them.

"At your service, Lord Commander. What is your will?"

"To fly to the south coast where there is a place we may not be seen. This is of high importance, and it must be done with speed. You are a pilot?"

"Of my father's personal craft, Lord Commander. But a scout—I have not flown one—" He was beginning when Turan interrupted him.

"Then you shall gather air time in one tonight. Battle comrade"—he turned now to Wamage—"for what you have done this night I can never give thanks enough. You have indeed saved my life, or at least lengthened it. Let that always be remembered between us."

"Let me go with you—" Wamage put out a hand as if to clutch Turan's arm.

"I leave you for a rear guard, one to cover me. It is a hard thing I ask of you—"

"But nothing that I will not do. Guard your back, Lord Commander!"

Ziantha was aware he watched her as he delivered that warning.

"Be sure I do," Turan answered.

They climbed aboard the strange flyer, and with the armsman for pilot the machine came to vibrating life, swung around, and ran along the field, until Ziantha was sure there was trouble and it would not lift.

With a bounce it did, and she felt queasy as she never had in a flitter. In the cramped cabin she could feel the vibration through her body. And it seemed to her that flying in this Forerunner world was a more rigorous experience than she had been accustomed to.

"It is fortunate, Lord Commander," their pilot said, "that these scouts have instant clearance from the field with no questioning by the control tower. Else—"

"Else we would have had a story for them," Turan said. "Now we can rather plan on landing. Listen well, for much depends upon this. You must set us down in a place as near to the sea as you can take this flyer. And it must be done with as little chance of discovery as possible. We are seeking a source of power, something which lies on an island and to which we have a single pointer. With this—with this—" Turan had hesitated and then began again, "I can promise the future will be changed."

But he did not say whose future. Ziantha smiled in the dark. Turan's—the real Turan's influence must be great—or had been great that he could bind these two men to his purposes. Though Wamage had had his doubts. Perhaps a sensitive in this civilization where the power was apparently so little known could apply pressure without even realizing it. Though she knew that if there was need she could control the armsman for a short time as she had Wamage.

"There is the Plateau of Xuth, Lord Commander. It—it has such an evil reputation that not many seek it out, not since the days of Lord Commander Rolphri, though that is all countryman's talk—"

Countryman's talk, maybe—Ziantha caught a hint or two of what lay in his mind as he spoke—but he believes it holds a threat. I pick up fear which is not of other men but of something strange. If Turan caught that also he would seem to discount it, for he replied promptly:

"Xuth is to our purpose. You can pilot us there?"

"I believe so, Lord Commander."

"Well enough." Turan had edged a little forward in his place. He was intent upon what the armsman was doing, and Ziantha knew that he was striving to pick up from the other the art of flying this ancient machine.

Had the alien mind-patterns been easier to contact he would have had no difficulty. But having to make allowances for constant disruption of mind-touch, his concentration must be forced to a higher level. Without his asking she began to feed him power, give him extra energy. Nor did she cease to marvel at his great endurance.

They did not speak again. Perhaps their pilot thought they slept. Once or twice they saw the riding lights of what must be other aircraft, but none came near, nor did there appear to be any pursuit. However, doubt nibbled at Ziantha's confidence. Surely they could not have got away from Singakok and the High Consort as easily as this!

The night sky grayed; they were coming into day. Dawn and then the full sunrise caught them. For the first time in hours the armsman spoke:

"The sea, Lord Commander. We turn south now to Xuth."

Turan was half collapsed in his seat. Ziantha regarded him with rising concern. His look of fatal illness was heightened by the sunlight. Could he last? And this was so faint a hope they followed— She fought the fear that uncoiled within her, began to seep coldly through her body.

"Xuth, Lord Commander. I can set down, I think, along this line."

In spite of her resolution Ziantha closed her eyes as the nose of the flyer tilted downward and the machine began a descent. It seemed so vulnerable, so dangerous, compared to the flitters that she could only hope the pilot knew what he was doing and they were not about to crash against some unyielding stretch of rock.

The machine touched ground, bounced, touched again with a jar that nearly shook Ziantha from her seat. She heard a gasp from Turan and looked to him. The gray cast on his face was more pronounced; his mouth was open as if he were gasping for breath. Although the flyer ran forward, the pilot's tension suggested he was fearing some further peril.

They stopped and the pilot exhaled so loudly she could hear him. "Fortune has favored us, Lord Commander."

Ziantha looked out. Ahead was only emptiness, as if they were close to the edge of some cliff, a deduction which proved true as they climbed out into a brisk, whipping breeze and the full sun of midmorning.

Beyond, Ziantha could hear the wash of sea surf, though there was more distance between the shore and the flyer than she had earlier believed. The pilot had landed on what was an amazingly level stretch of rock running like an avenue between tall monoliths and crags of rock.

There was no vegetation to be seen, and those standing stones were of an unrelieved black, though the surface on which they stood was of a red-veined gray rock. A sudden sobbing wail brought an answering cry from her, as she whirled about to face the direction from which that had come.

"Wind—in the rocks," Turan's voice, strained but no longer only a gasp.

But she wondered. Her sensitive's reaction to this place was sharp. As the armsman had hinted—there was evil here. She would not want to touch any of those strange black rocks, read what they held imprisoned in them. For there was such a sense of the past here—an alien past—as one might gather from the walls of a tomb, entirely inimical to all her life force. Those were not just rocks, standing upright because wind and erosion had whittled them so. No, they were alien, had been placed there for a purpose. Ruins—a long vanished city—a temple—Ziantha did not want to know which.

There were birds with brilliant yellow wings flashing in the sunlight out over the sea. But none approached the cliff edge, nor were there any droppings from roosts among the near stones, as if living things shunned Xuth. Ziantha probed Vintra's memory and received a troubled response. Xuth—yes, it had been known to the rebel. But only as a legend, a haunted place wherein some defeat of the past had over-turned all rule and order and from which had sprung many of the ills of this world, ills which had festered until this latter-day rebellion had burst in turn.

Now she tested not Vintra's memory but her own talent. So much could influence that. Not only the weather, emo-tions, the very geography of the site, but also subtle emana-tions of her surroundings. Would that very ancient evil, which was like a faint, sickening odor in the nostrils, work to com-bat what she must do?

Keeping well away from any contact with the rocks, Ziantha went on toward the sound of the sea, coming out on a ledge that projected like the beginning of a long-lost bridge over the surf which constantly assaulted the wall below. There was no sign of any beach; the meeting of cliff and water displayed wicked teeth of smaller rocks, around which the sea washed with intimidating force.

But here, on this prong, she was free of the darkness the black monoliths radiated. If there was any place from which she could search the sea it was here where the spray rose high enough in the air to be borne inland, leaving a spattering of moisture along the ledge.

Having won freedom from that other influence, Ziantha felt she dared not return to it. Here and now she must make her attempt to find their guide.

"Here," she mind-sent. "There is too much residue of some

old ill among the stones. I can only do this thing free of them."

"I am coming—"

She turned to watch him moving slowly, with such care as if he must plan and then enforce each movement of his body, none of which were instinctive now. He had waved back the pilot who remained by the flyer. And when he reached her his head was up, his eyes steady and clear.

"You are ready?"

"As much as I shall ever be." Now that the final moment before carrying out her decision had come she wanted to flee it. She had used the focus-stone to its full power before, and it had brought her here. When she used it again—where would it take her? And would the change be as entire, as binding, as it now was? She had the gem in her hand, but before she looked into it, surrendered to the talent, Ziantha made a last appeal.

"Anchor me. Do not let me be lost. For if I am—"

"We both are." He nodded. "I shall give you all I have to give, be sure of that."

"Then—" she cupped the stone between her hands, raised it to her forehead—

The sea, the pound of the sea—wild, raging—the devouring sea! Around her the tower room trembled, the air was filled with the thunder of the waters. The anger of the sea against Nornoch. Would these walls stand through this storm? And if they did—what of the next and the next—?

Ziantha—no, who was Ziantha? A name—a faint flash of memory to which she tried to cling even as it vanished, as a dream vanishes upon waking. D'Eyree!

"D'Eyree!" her voice rang above the clamor of the storm, as if she summoned herself from sleep to face what must come.

She raised her hands uncertainly before her. Surely she

should have been holding something—on the floor—look! The urgency, the fear of loss gripped her, sent her to her knees, her hands groping across the thick carpet.

Her every movement brought a clash, a jangling from the strings of polished shells which formed her skirt, just as they fashioned the tight, scant bodice which barely covered her flat breasts. Her skin—green, pale green, or gold—or blue—no, that color came from the scales which covered her, like small dim jewels laid edge to edge.

She was D'Eyree of the Eyes. The Eyes!

No longer did she run her hands across the floor in vain search. She had had such a foolish thought. Where would the Eyes be but where they had always rested since the Choosing made her what she was? She raised her fingers now to touch that band about her forehead with the two gems she could not see, only feel, one above each temple, just as they should be. How could she have thought them lost?

She was D'Eyree and—

She was—Ziantha! A flooding of memory, like a fire to cleanse the mist in her mind. Her head snapped up and she looked around at strangeness.

The walls of the oval room were opaline, with many soft colors playing across them, and they were very smooth as might be a shell's interior. The carpet on the floor was rusty red, soft and springy with a queer life of its own.

There were two windows, long and narrow slits. She went hastily to the nearest. She was Ziantha—no, D'Eyree! The Eyes—they fought to make her D'Eyree. She willed her hands to pull at the band that bound them to her head. Her fingers combed coarse hair like thick seaweed but could not move that band.

Ziantha must hold to Ziantha—learn where Nornoch might be.

She looked out, ducking as spray from the storm-driven waves fell salty on her face. But she glimpsed the other towers; this portion of Nornoch was guardian to the land behind, where she was warden.

Only, the sea was winning; after all these centuries it was winning. Her people held this outpost, and when the Three Walls were breached, when the sea came again—they would be swept away, back and down, to become, if any survived, what they had once been; mindless living things of the under-ooze. But that—that would not be! Not while the Eyes had a voice, a mind! Six eyes and their wearers—one for each wall still.

She leaned against the slit, a hand to each side of it, fighting for calm. Bringing all the power which was D'Eyree's by both inheritance and training to subdue this stranger in her mind, she put her—it—away and concentrated on that which was her mission, to will the walls to hold, to be one with the defense.

Think of her wall, of how the creatures, the Lurla, had built it and the two others from secretions of their own bodies over the centuries, of how those creatures had been fed and tended, bred and cherished by the people of Nornoch to create defenses against the sea. *Will* the Lurla to work, now—will!—will! She was no longer even D'Eyree; she was a will, a call to action so that creatures stirred sluggishly, began to respond. Ah, so slowly! Yet they could not be prodded to any greater efforts or speed.

Secrete, build, strengthen—that Nornoch not yield! Move, so that the waves do not eat us into nothingness again. The Eyes—let the power that is in the Eyes goad the Lurla to awake and work.

But so few! Was that because, as D'Fani said, her people had dared turn away from the old ways—the sacrifices? Will— she must not let her thoughts, her concentration stray from what was to be done. Lurla—she could see them in her mind —their sluglike bodies as they crawled back and forth across the wall which was her own responsibility, leaving behind them ever those trails of froth that hardened on contact with the air and steadily became another layer within the buttress foundations of the Three Walls, the towers. Stir, Lurla! Awake, move—do this for the life of Nornoch!

But they were more sluggish than they had ever been. Two dropped from the walls, lay inert. What was—? D'Eyree raised her hands from the walls, pressed her palms to the Eyes, feeling their chill.

Awake, Lurla! This is no time to sleep. The storm is high; do you not feel the tower shake? Awake, crawl, build!

Lurla—it was as if she raised her voice to shriek that aloud.

The sea's pound was in her ears, but fainter, its fury lessened. Then D'Fani was wrong; this was not one of the great storms after all. She need not have feared—

"Ziantha!"

There was no window through which she looked. She was in the open with a bird's screams sounding above the surf. And before her, hands on her shoulders (as if those hands had dragged her out of the time and place that had been), Turan.

She wrested herself from his grip to wheel about on the rock, face out over the waves, straining as if she could from this point catch a glimpse of Nornoch, learn whether its towers, the Three Walls, were still danger-wrapped, if the Lurla had been kept to their task.

No, that was all finished long ago. How long? Her talent could not answer that. Perhaps as many years stood now between D'Eyree and Vintra as between Vintra and Ziantha. And that number her mind reeled from calculating.

Only now she knew where Nornoch lay, if any of Nornoch still survived. That much they had gained. She pointed with an outflung hand.

"Over sea—or under it—but there!" She spoke aloud, for the burden of weariness which followed upon a trance lay on her. And she allowed Turan to take her hand, draw her back to the flyer.

As if their coming was a signal, the armsman came out of the cabin. Beneath his close-fitting helmet hood his face was anxious.

"Lord Commander, I have had it on the wave-speak. They are using S-Code—"

Vintra's memory identified that for her and, lest Turan's memory no longer served him, Ziantha supplied what she knew by mind-touch. "A military code of top security."

"The rebels—" Turan began.

But the armsman shook his head. "Lord Commander, I was com officer for my unit. They hunt you and—they have orders to shoot you down!"

There was a look of misery on his young face, as if the first shock had worn off so he could believe, even if he did not understand.

"Zuha must be desperate," Ziantha commented.

"It does not matter. Only time matters," Turan returned. "Battle comrade, here we must part company. You have served me better than you will ever know. However I cannot take you with us farther—"

"Lord Commander, wherever you go, then I shall fly you!" His determination was plain.

"Not to Nornoch—" What made Ziantha say that she did not know.

His head jerked around. "What—what do you know of Nornoch?"

"That it holds what we seek," she answered.

"Lord Commander, do not let her! Nornoch—that is a story—a tale of the sea that sailors have used to frighten their children since the beginning. There is no Nornoch, no fish-people, except in evil dreams!"

"Then in dreams we must seek it."

The armsman moved between them and the cabin of the

flyer. "Lord Commander, this—this rebel has indeed bewitched you. Do not let her lead you to your death!"

Tired as she was Ziantha did what must be done, centering her power, thrusting it at him as she might have thrust with a primitive spear or sword. His hands went to his head; he gave a moaning cry and stumbled back, away, until he wilted to the ground well beyond the wing shadow of the flyer.

"Ill done," she said, "but there was naught else—"

"I know," Turan said, his voice as flat, sounding as tired as she felt. "We must go before he revives. Where we go we cannot take him. You are sure of the course?"

"I am sure," she answered steadily as they climbed into the cabin.

11

Ziantha wanted to close her eyes as Turan brought the flyer's engines to life and headed toward the sea. Would the craft lift into the sky, or would they lose altitude and be licked down by the hungry waves below? That he had learned all he could from the pilot, she knew, but his first flight alone might be his last. They were out—over the water —and for a heart-shaking moment, Ziantha thought they had failed. Then the nose of the flyer came up. There was a terrible look of strain on Turan's gaunt face, as if by will alone he lifted them into the sky.

She held the focus-stone cupped in her hands, ever aware of the thread of force which pulled. But where lay the other Eye now? Beneath the ocean where they could not find it?

She concentrated on that guide, being careful, however, not to let the stone draw her into a trance. And to keep that delicate balance of communication between the focus and the retention of her own identity was exhausting. Also her strength of body was beginning to fail. She was aware of hunger, of thirst, of the need for sleep, and she willed these away from her, employing techniques Ogan had long drilled into her to use her body as a tool and not allow its demands to rise paramount.

How far? That was of the greatest importance. The flyer might not be fueled for a long trip. And if they could not land when they reached their goal—what then?

Ziantha kept her mind closed, asked no questions of

Turan, knowing that his failing strength was now centered on getting them to their goal. And her part was that of guide.

Time was no longer measured. But the girl became aware that that thread which had been so slight on their setting forth from land was growing stronger, easier to sense. And with that realization her confidence arose. The stone was growing warmer, and she glanced at it quickly. Its brilliance had increased and it gave off flashes of light, as if it were a communication device.

"The stone," she spoke aloud, not using mind-touch lest she disturb his concentration, "it is coming to life!"

"Then we must be near—" His voice was very low, hardly above a whisper.

But if the sea covered—

Ziantha moved closer to the vision port, tried to see ahead. The sun's reflection from the waves was strong but— A dark shadow, rising from the sea!

"Turan, an island!"

The flyer circled it. What Ziantha could see was forbidding; jagged spires of rock, no vegetation. Where could they land? Had this been a flitter of their own time and world they would need only a reasonably open space to set down. But she had seen the take-off of these ancient machines and knew they required much more.

As Turan circled he spoke:

"It is larger than I expected. Either the report was wrong, or more of it has arisen since the first upheaval."

"Look!" Ziantha cried. "To the south—there!"

A stretch of great blocks of masonry locked together, stretching from the cliffs of the inner portion of the island out into the waves. Those dashed against it, leaving it wet with spray. It might have been a pier fashioned to accommodate a whole fleet of vessels.

"Can you land on that?"

"There is one way of proving it." And it would seem Turan was desperate enough to try.

This time Ziantha did shut her eyes as he banked and turned to make the run along that strange sea-wet roadway, if road it was. She felt the jarring impact of their first touch, the bumps and bounces as they hurtled along a surface that was plainly not as smooth as it had appeared from the air. Then the vibration of the motor died. They came to a stop without crashing against a rock or diving headlong into the waiting waves.

When she dared to look she saw the vision port wet with spray. The flyer rocked slightly under the pound of water, diffused though that was by the time it reached them. They were safely down.

"Turan!" She glanced around. He had slumped in his seat. She caught his shoulder, shook him. "Turan!"

He turned his head with painful slowness. There was the starkness of death in his eyes.

"I cannot hold—much longer— Listen, open your mind!"

Stiff with fear, she dropped the focus-stone into her lap so that no emanation of that could befog reception for her and leaned forward, set her hands on either side of his head, held it, as if he were some artifact she must read for her life's sake.

Information flooded into her mind—all he had picked up from the armsman, how to fly them away when what she had come to do was finished, and what she must do afterward if she were successful here.

She accepted this. Then she protested:

"Hold fast! You must hold fast. For if you cannot—then—"

To be entrapped here forever! In a way that was worse than death. Or would death free him when it took back the body it had never fully released to life? Ziantha did not know. All she was sure of was that she could not allow him to die here. That she must, if she could, not only find the key for her return, but also for his.

She leaned closer to him, and instinct moved her to another kind of touch, one that carried in it the seeds of vigorous life as her kind knew it. As her lips met his cold, flaccid ones, she willed her energy into him.

"Hold!"

But there was so little time. Ziantha struggled with the catch on the cabin door, forced it open, stepped out. She cupped the focus-stone to her breast and started back along the causeway. From the air it had looked shorter than it was. The flyer had come to a halt about halfway along it, and there was a wide stretch to traverse before she would reach the sharp rise of the main portion of the island.

It was plain that this roadway was not natural but the work of hands, and also that it had been long under the sea. It was encrusted with shells, and there were patches of decaying water weeds still rooted to it. The stones from which it was fashioned were huge blocks, some fully the size of the flyer in length, and so well set together that even the centuries and the sea had not pulled one from the other.

The draw of the focus-stone was now so strong that she felt as if a real cord was looped about the gem dragging her forward. Somewhere ahead lay the other end of that cord. But where in that maze of rock could it be?

Her road ended in a jumble of huge blocks, as if some structure had been shaken down there, yet the focus still pulled. Ziantha began a painful climb in and among the stones. The clothing she wore had never been intended for such usage. And her knees were scraped and bleeding after two unlucky falls, two of her fingernails torn to the quick, her palm gashed by a sharp shell edge.

But she fought her way on and up that mountain of tumbled stone until she reached a point above. And there—

Although the cord continued to pull there was no further advance. For before her was another of the incredibly ancient structures, only this had no break. It was a smooth wall projecting from the cliff behind it.

Ziantha ran her bleeding hand across its surface, seeking an opening her eyes might not be able to detect; there was nothing to meet her touch. Yet she knew that behind this lay what she sought. With a whimper of despair, the girl sank down at the foot of the wall. Her hands could not tear a way through that. Perhaps there was some weapon or tool in the flyer—but she doubted it. This masonry which had withstood sea burial for centuries could not easily be broached.

There was only one way, and she dreaded it. She could not depend on any backing. To call upon Turan to support her through a trance might mean his death. Yet she must take this final step, or they would fail, and failure would mean they would end here. That inborn spark of refusal to accept death without a struggle that was the heritage of her own species stiffened her resolution. She set the focus-stone to her forehead.

Once more she was in that nacre-walled room. The Eyes in their band rested heavy on her forehead, just as a weariness which was of the spirit as well as of the body weighed on her heavily. There was fear as dark about her as if shadows drew in from the gleaming walls to smother her.

The storm—she had lasted out the storm, kept the Lurla to their labor of strengthening the walls—but just barely. They had resisted—resisted! With a small hiss of breath she faced what that meant. Her power, her control over the Eyes, must be fading. And it was time for her—

No! It was not time! She was not that old, that weak! The storm had been greater than any they had known before, that was all. And the Lurla had tired. It was not her control slipping. She looked down at her still-rounded body, firm under the veiling of her shell-string clothing. No, she was not ready

133

to put off the Eyes, to take the next remorseless and inevitable step her abdication would lead to.

D'Eyree crossed to the window slit. Now storm-driven waves had subsided for this time. Still the sea looked sullen, angry, and even the tint of the sky was ominous. If the calculations of D'Ongi were right—

Through the sighing of the sea, she heard a slight sound behind her, turned to face a woman standing at a door that had opened in the apparently seamless wall. She was slight, her coarse hair the darkest green of youth. Her body was bare, sleek, and glistening from recent immersion in the sea, her neck gills still a little open.

"Honor to the Eyes," the woman said, but there was mockery in that hail. "There is good gleaning in the storm leavings. Also, D'Huna has spoken—she finds the burden of the Eyes now beyond her power."

And all the time she watched D'Eyree with cruel and greedy eyes.

Ah, yes, D'Atey, how much you wish that I would also resign this power! D'Eyree forced herself not to put hand to the Eye band. D'Atey, you have never rested content since the Eyes came to me and not to you, and you have so carefully provided that your sister-kin will have the next chance to stand for warden. But D'Huna—she is five seasons younger than I! And that will be remembered. I am not loved too greatly in Nornoch. It has been my way to walk a lone path. Yet that I cannot alter, for it is a part of me. Only now—who will stand to my back if clamor grows?

"D'Huna has served well." Carefully she schooled her voice. This one must not suspect she had scored with her news.

"She may serve even better." A pointed tongue showed, caressed D'Atey's lips as if she savored some taste and would prolong that pleasure. "There is a meeting of the warriors' council—"

134

D'Eyree stiffened and then forced herself to relax, hoping that the other had not seen that momentary betrayal of emotion, though she feared that nothing escaped those vicious, envious eyes of D'Atey's.

"Such is not by custom. The Eyes did not attend—"

"D'Fani holds by the Law of Triple Danger. In such times the warriors are independent of the Eyes. That, too, is custom."

D'Eyree, by great effort, bit back an exclamation. D'Fani who was the fanatic, the believer in the old dark ways the people had set aside—D'Fani who talked of the Feeding— If D'Fani gained followers enough what might happen?

"They meet now, the warriors." D'Atey moved a little closer, her eyes still searching D'Eyree's face for some sign of concern. "D'Fani speaks to them. Also the Voice of the Peak—"

"The Voice of the Peak," D'Eyree interrupted her, "has not uttered for as many years as you have been hatched, D'Atey. D'Rubin himself could not make it answer when he worked upon its inner parts this past year. The ancients had their secrets and we have lost them."

"Not so many as we thought were lost. And perhaps it was because we sought other paths, less hard ones, weaker ones. But D'Tor has found a way to make the Voice utter. He follows his brother in seeking the wisdom of the old ways. Rumor says now our future will be shortened if we do not find a way to rebreed the Lurla. D'Huna failed with three during the storm."

Three? She had failed to spur *three!* But there had been *four* that resisted D'Eyree. And D'Huna had resigned the Eyes. Thus it would follow that she must also— But what had D'Atey earlier hinted at? She must know more.

"You spoke of D'Huna serving better." She hated to ask a question of D'Atey; there was a gloating about the other which fed her own inner fear. "What mean you by that?"

"If the Voice foretells another storm, then D'Fani will have a powerful voice in the council. Are the Eyes not vowed for their lifetime to the service of Nornoch? How better can they serve, once their power over the Lurla has waned, than to provide strength for the Lurla to procreate in greater abundance? Once the Feeding was custom. It is only the weaklings of these latter days who want it set aside—"

This time D'Eyree could not control her slight hiss of breath, though she writhed inwardly a second later when she saw the flash of triumph in D'Atey's eyes.

"The Feeding was of the old days, when the people followed dark customs. There is the Pledge of D'Gan that we be no longer barbarians of the dark. Have we risen from the muck to choose once more to live in it?"

"D'Fani believes that our weakness in listening to D'Gan and his like has doomed us. How find you the Lurla, Eyes Wearer? Are they as strong, as obedient to your orders as they have always been?"

D'Eyree forced a smile. "Ask that of Nornoch, D'Atey. Has a tower tumbled? Have the walls cracked in any storm?"

"Not this time perhaps. But if the Voice says there will be a second storm, a third—" Now D'Atey smiled. "I think after D'Huna's report, D'Fani will have many listening to him. He may even call for a trial of power, D'Eyree. Think you well on that."

She nodded and slipped away. D'Eyree looked once more to the sea. The Voice—had D'Fani's brother really repaired it? Or was it, as more likely, some trick of D'Fani's to influence the council and the people to plunge back into the old ways from which D'Gan had raised them? The Voice was set on the highest peak within the Three Walls. In the old days it had predicted accurately the coming of storms. But custom had been its conqueror. For by custom only one line of the people serviced the Voice, understood its intricate mechanism. And when the Plague of the Red Tide Year had struck, those who had understood the Voice had been, for some reason, the first stricken.

For years it had continued to operate even though those who had once tended it were gone. And the people had been lulled into believing that it was indestructible. Then it slowed, became inaccurate by days with its warnings. Finally it stopped. Though men had labored for two generations now to relearn its workings, they had been uniformly unsuccessful. The belief had been held for a long time that, like the Lurla, the Voice answered to mental control—a control inherited by the one clan that no longer existed. There were no visible focus points of communication to be discovered, nothing like the Eyes.

The Eyes—and D'Huna had surrendered hers! Perhaps she had surrendered even more as D'Atey had suggested. Of course the Lurla no longer bred as they once did. But their number had always been carefully controlled as was needful. However, suppose that a mutant strain had developed, one not so quick to answer to the dominance of the Eyes? The people had changed over the centuries since they had ventured forth step by step from the sea. They were amphibians now. But the fear had always hung over them that if they were forced out of Nornoch, which was their grip upon the land, they would lose their hard-won intelligence and revert again to sea creatures who could not think of themselves as human.

To return to feeding the Lurla on food long forbidden—could that be right? D'Gan had taught that such practices were savage, reducing those who held them to the status of one of the fanged sea raiders.

The band that held the Eyes seemed to press so tightly on D'Eyree's forehead that it was a burden weighting her head; she could not carry it proudly aloft as became her. She returned to the window slit, resting her head against its solid frame, the breeze from the sea cool and moist against her scaled skin. She was so tired. Let those who had never worn the Eyes, carried that burden, think of the powers and privileges of her position. The weight, fear, and responsibility of it was far heavier than any respect could bolster.

Why then not follow D'Huna, admit that the Lurla had been sluggish for her, that four had failed? But if she did that, she was surrendering another kind of wall to D'Fani and those who followed him. The only possible wearers of the Eyes were very young, easily influenced, and one was D'Wasa, whom D'Eyree did not trust.

No, as long as she could, she must not surrender to her weariness, the more so if the Feeding returned. Not only did her whole being shrink from the very thought of that horror for herself; she knew it would also be throwing open the gate to the worst of the people.

Yet if the Voice proclaimed another such storm ahead, and D'Fani called for a trial of power before that came—

She was like one swimming between a fanged raider and a many-arms, with cause to believe that each was alerted to her passing and ready to put an end to her. And she was so tired—

D'Huna—she would go to D'Huna. She must know more of the failure of the Lurla—whether the other believed what she herself suspected, that it was not the fault of the Eyes, but of a mutation in the Lurla themselves. Knowledge was strength and the more knowledge she could garner the better she could build her own defense.

Even if D'Huna had surrendered her Eyes, she would not have left her tower. That by custom she could not do until the new wearer entered into it and took formal possession. So there was yet time.

D'Eyree threaded a way along nacre-walled corridors, climbed down in one section, up in another. The majority of the people never came into these link-ways between the towers. The privacy of the wearers was well guarded, lest they be disturbed at some time when it was necessary to check upon the Lurla or otherwise use their talent. And with a council in progress and the possibility of the Voice making some pronouncement, the attention of most of Nornoch would be centered elsewhere.

She passed no one during her journey; the towers might be deserted. Though there were six wearers on permanent duty, two for each wall. If D'Caquk and D'Lov had heard the news, there was no indication they stirred to hear more. The pale glow of the in-lights shone above their doors as she passed. Then she came to D'Huna's tower.

With her webbed fingers D'Eyree rapped out their private call code. Slowly, almost reluctantly, the slit door opened, and she stepped into a room the duplicate of her own. D'Huna faced her, looking strange without the Eyes. D'Eyree had never seen her without them since they had become wearers on the same day.

"Kin-close," D'Eyree spoke first, a little daunted by the unfocused stare the other turned on her—as if D'Eyree were not there at all. "I have been told a tale I cannot believe." Her voice trailed away.

"What can you not believe?" D'Huna asked in a voice as lacking in animation as her face. "That I have put aside the Eyes, that I am no longer one to watch and ward? If it is of that you speak, it is the truth."

"But why have you done this thing? All—all of us know that the Lurla can be sluggish at times, that it is hard to drive them to their task. Of late years this has grown more and more the case."

"With the storm," D'Huna did not answer her directly, "I learned what the Lurla have become. Three would not answer the Eyes, even when I used the full force of my will. Therefore I failed Nornoch by so much. Let another who can bring more force to bear take my place, lest the wall crack at last."

"Are you sure that another can do better?"

At that sharp question life showed in D'Huna's face; there

was a flicker in her large eyes. She stared at D'Eyree as if she still wore the Eyes, was attempting to bring their strength to bear on her sister wearer, to read her thoughts.

"What do you mean?" she asked.

"Have you sensed no difference in the Lurla?" D'Eyree might be grasping now for a small scrap of hope, but if she could make D'Huna question her own self-judgment perhaps there was a way out for them all. "As I have said, they have been sluggish of late. Perhaps it is not that our powers fail, but that the Lurla are more armored against us."

"Be that so—then it will be also said that the Feeding once made them obey, that without it they are beyond our holding. Let another who is newly trained, perhaps stronger, stand in my place and try."

The Feeding! So D'Huna was half converted to that belief. But did she not understand the danger in allowing that thought to spread? Perhaps she, D'Eyree, should keep to herself the observations she had made, or she would be giving ammunition to the enemy.

But even as she reflected, D'Huna's expression changed. She threw off that blankness and her interest awakened.

"So—you have found them sluggish. Tell me—how many failed *you* this time!"

"Why should you—"

"Why should I think that?" D'Huna countered. "Because you are afraid, D'Eyree. Yes, I can read it in you, this fear. You sought me out, wishing to learn why I put off the Eyes. That being so, I think that it follows that you have also found your power failing you. There is no place for a wearer whom the Eyes fail. Would you be humbled before all the people by being forced to a trial? Set aside the Eyes by your own will; let them not be torn from you so that all may see a piteous thing worthy of contempt!"

"It is not so easy." D'Eyree longed to deny the other's accusation. But one cannot tell untruths to a wearer. "D'Fani speaks with the council. He urges a return to the Feeding; he promises the Voice will speak—"

"Suppose that it does and it tells of another storm such as that just past? And suppose a wearer who no longer has full power strives to keep the Lurla to their task and fails—shall Nornoch then fall because of her pride?"

"It is not pride, no—nor fear, save a little," D'Eyree protested. "If we revert to the Feeding, then, I believe, it is better we quickly, cleanly, return through wind and wave to that which brought us forth, not sink back by degrees, forgetting all D'Gan taught. For the Feeding is evil, that I believe above all!"

"Which is strange coming from one sworn to nurture the Lurla above even her own life!" It was a man's voice.

D'Eyree spun around to face the speaker.

D'Fani! she shaped his name with her lips but did not utter it aloud.

12

He stood there arrogantly, taller than most other males, if less robust of body. His quick, dominant mind blazed through his eyes. At that moment D'Eyree in a flash of intuition knew what made him a threat to her and all her kind. D'Fani had part of the power, not as the wearers had it, but enough so he resented that he had not the right to the Eyes. Because he lacked them he was her enemy.

D'Fani was no warrior either. He was inept with any weapon save his tongue and his mind. But those he had sharpened to his use so that he had gained ascendancy over others with greater strength. In their world he had carved a place, now he aspired to a greater one.

In this moment of their eyes' meeting, D'Eyree knew this. Now she not only feared for herself, and vaguely for Nornoch; she feared for a way of life that D'Fani would destroy so that he might rule.

"You are sworn to defend the Lurla," he repeated when she made no answer. "Is that not so, Eye Wearer?" There was in him that same strain of cruel maliciousness which D'Atey showed, save that here it was a hundred times the worse.

"I am sworn so," D'Eyree answered steadily. "I am also sworn to the way of D'Gan." Her future might be forfeit now. She had feared such a meeting, yet at this moment she drew upon some inner strength she had not known she possessed.

"If the Lurla die, then where do the precepts of a man already long dead lead us?" He had assumed the mask of someone being reasonable with a child or one of little under-standing. But D'Fani classed all females as such.

To argue with him was folly; she could make no impres-sion, that she knew. And that he would force a trial on her was probable. Would any of the other wearers support her? She thought that she dared not count on that, not after this exchange with D'Huna. It would seem she had dragged disas-ter upon herself by this impulsive visit here. But, that being so, she must waste no time in regrets but turn her whole mind to the struggle D'Fani would make her face. As much time as she had—

Time? Something dim, a wisp of memory stirred deep in her mind—a strange memory she did not understand. Time was important, not only to her but to someone else— Just as in that flash D'Fani's motives had been clear for her to read, so now did she have an instant of otherness—a sensation of being another person. It was frightening, and her hands went to her forehead, to press above the Eyes.

What had she seen, felt, in that moment of disorientation? It was gone, yet it left behind a residue of feeling, of urgency that she must accomplish some necessary act. With the tech-niques of a wearer she willed that away. Only D'Fani was important now.

"Do those weigh heavily upon you, Wearer?" he de-manded. "There is a remedy. Put them off. Or would you have them taken from you for failure, after proof before the people that the Lurla will no longer answer you?"

"There can be no such proof!" She held her head high. That teasing memory-which-was-not-true was gone. "Who are you to presume to judge a wearer's fitness?"

She was reckless, excited, as if she were forced to challenge him so that no more time would be wasted. And her words reacted on him as one of the mind-thrusts did upon a Lurla. He did not visibly twist under it, but the color of his scaled flesh deepened.

"There is one way to judge a wearer—a trial. And since D'Huna has relinquished her Eyes, there is already one arranged. It would seem you will have a part in it also."

Did he expect her to beg off? If so he would be disappointed. Half-consciously she had known this would be the end. Her voice was still even and controlled as she answered:

"So be it, then."

Whatever mission had brought him to D'Huna's quarters seemed forgotten as, with a gloating look at D'Eyree, he left. When he was gone D'Eyree turned to the other woman.

"You gave him an open door when you put aside the Eyes."

"And you gave him another," D'Huna replied. "I was obeying the law when I could no longer control the Lurla. If you do no better, then the longer you hold the Eyes, the more you are at fault."

"And if D'Fani sweeps the council and the people with him back to the old dark ways? Do you not remember the Chronicles of the Wearers—who were the first to be subjected to the Feeding? Are you martyr enough to ask for that? How much better can D'Fani make plain his power than by such a spectacle?"

"We vowed when we put on the Eyes to abide by the law—"

D'Eyree flung out one hand in an impatient gesture. "Do not quote law to me—not when it means the Feeding! Not when it serves D'Fani to climb to the rulership of Nornoch! Though do not fear—if he has his will *I* shall furnish the banquet—not you."

She turned her back on the other; any more words between them would give D'Fani weapons to use against her. And she was not what she had accused D'Huna of being, a willing martyr.

Back she went to her own tower, trying to think, to control those fears D'Fani brought to her mind. But it was when she looked from the sea-window that she was shocked out of her preoccupation. There were the signs she had been trained to read—another storm was on the way.

For one to follow so quickly upon the last was unnatural. And the Lurla were tired; they should have rest, the nourishment of their specially grown food. Also—D'Huna's section of the wall now had no warden.

The Lurla— D'Eyree used the Eyes to look into their burrows. They lay flaccid, thick rolls of boneless flesh, upon the flooring. There was not even a twitching. She tried a thought probe. One—two—raised their fore-ends a little. The rest lay supine, inert. And they did not have that bloated look of afterfeeding.

For the first time D'Eyree did then what it was against all custom to do. She allowed her thought-sight to invade the Lurla pens of the other wearers. In each she noted those which seemed well fed, but there were a far greater number who were not. And some of those in the other pens were moving restlessly, angrily. If this were reported—more fuel for D'Fani!

Her weather-wise eyes told her there was perhaps a day before the storm gathered to full strength. Long enough for D'Fani to strike. There was nothing she could do—or was there?

The Lurla were fed on cultures blended by a time-tested formula devised by D'Gan. But before that— She used the Eyes again in a manner she had never tried before, not certain whether they could so serve her, not to watch, to encourage the Lurla—but rather to trace through the walls and the rock of this island certain ancient channels she knew of only by tradition. And to her relief she found she could do this.

Heartened by her first success, D'Eyree explored farther and farther, concentrating on those hidden ways so they also formed pictures in her mind. At last she found the outer gate, and it did give into the sea, well under the surface waves. Now—

D'Eyree gathered her power. There was plenty of life force in the water, though she could not distinguish the separate forms which emitted it, only the impact of the life itself. She began to use thought even as she used it to send the Lurla to labor. But this time she strove to entice, to draw it after her as a fisherman pulls a loaded net.

She played, angled, worked with concentration. In hardly daring to believe that she was succeeding, D'Eyree retraced those long forgotten and unused inner tunnels, bringing the life down them, and so into those pools where the culture for feeding was kept. Three times she made the awesome journey from the sea to the pool by which the Lurla sprawled inertly.

How much life she had so snared she could not tell, save that the vigorous force of it registered. Now D'Eyree turned her attention to one of the unfed Lurla—that nearest to the pool. As she would urge it to work during the storm, she used her talent as a lash to push it toward the pool. It moved weakly, as if so far spent that the least effort exhausted it, but it did move.

Then—

It had reached the pool side. There was a quiver of interest, of awakening. A moment or so later she knew that the first part of her experiment was working. The Lurla was aroused to feed, and it was absorbing the life force.

Not only that but the radiation of its satisfaction was reaching its fellows. They were beginning to crawl toward the pool, to share the feast. Exhausted, she threw herself on the soft carpet, sundering contact with the Lurla in order to strengthen her control. If the Lurla fed well and throve on the bounty of the sea, then D'Fani would be answered and would not dare propose the Feeding. They need only activate the old food tunnels. Of course, in time they would face the same problem which D'Gan's generation had known before them: the inability to continue to feed the Lurla with natural food in quantity enough to build up their strength, especially after great storms had driven the sea dwellers into the depths. But a breathing space in which to defeat D'Fani's immediate plans was all she wanted now.

Time—

Again she was shaken by an uncurling of strange memory. Something far buried in her clamored for expression. D'Eyree sat up, drawing her bent knees close to her breast, her arms about them, huddling in upon herself as she battled with that part of her mind that seemed to be an invader. There was no time— Why did that haunt her so? Yet she would not explore behind that thought; she was afraid to do so with a fear as deadly as her distrust of D'Fani.

A sound—it echoed, vibrated through the walls of the tower—through her body.

The Voice! It had never been heard in her lifetime, but there was no mistaking it for anything else. D'Fani had in so much backed his boasts—the Voice was speaking.

No words, just the rhythm of its beat. But that entered into one's body, one's mind! D'Eyree cried out. For the vibration centered in the Eyes, and they caused such a blaze of pain that she rolled across the floor, now whimpering in gasps of agony, clawing at the band that held the source of torture against her skull.

Somehow she got it loose, dragged it off. Then she lay panting, the relief so great she could only grasp that the pain was gone. Still the beat of the Voice shook her bone and flesh, and somehow its meaning was clear in her mind.

As she had drawn that life force in the sea to feed the Lurla, just so was she being drawn. Yet something within her, some hard core which was herself, D'Eyree, was still firm against that pull. And random thoughts drew together.

In all the tales of the Voice she had never heard of this effect. This was something different—wrong. The Voice was a warning, a defense for the people. It did not beat down the mind, control one. What had D'Fani done to unleash this?

Wrong, all wrong! The realization of that was strong inside her. This was a tampering, an assault— Still, even as she thought that she was crawling against her will on hands and knees toward the door in answer to the summons of that unending sound.

No, she would not answer the Voice—this Voice that was D'Fani's weapon. D'Eyree fought against the compulsion until she lay writhing on the floor. The band of the Eyes was about one arm like a giant's bracelet that did not fit, now she brought it to her. The Eyes were braziers filled with blue-green fire, as she had never seen them before. To loose the compulsion—could she touch them, then focus her power on breaking the call of the Voice?

The pain—could she stand it? With courage she did not know she had, D'Eyree laid her hands across the Eyes. Pain, yes, but not so intense, not so concentrated as when she wore them.

She could stand this, and the very hurt helped to break the drag of the Voice. If she went, and she believed she must see what was happening, then she would be armed by having her own will back.

She took the way from the tower inward to the heart of Nornoch. People moved along it with her. But none spoke to the others; rather they stared straight ahead in such concentration as she herself knew when she worked with the Lurla.

So they came to the heart of Nornoch, that tallest spur of rock which had never been leveled, on which was hung the Voice in its cage. And on the ledge beneath it was D'Fani. His entire head was encased in a transparent arg shell of vast size. And below him were D'Atey and others, similarly shielded against the sound of the Voice.

But the people stood swaying in time to the beat of that sound from above. And their faces were blank, without expression. Closer and closer they moved to the foot of that spur, packed tightly now, yet those on the fringe still pushed as if it were imperative that they reach the Voice itself.

D'Eyree halted where she was, keeping her hold on reality with her grip on the Eyes. But she saw faces she knew in that throng. Not only D'Huna, who had divested herself of her Eyes, but the other wearers, and none wore their bands of office.

She looked from them to D'Fani above. There was a vast exultation on his face as his head turned slowly from side to side. He might be numbering those gathered below, taking pleasure in their subordination to the device.

D'Eyree moved back, but she was too late. He saw her and at the same instant was aware that the spell of the Voice did not hold her in thrall. Leaning forward, he caught at the shoulder of one of the helmeted guards below him, pointing with his other hand to D'Eyree.

As the guard raised a distance harpoon, D'Eyree turned and ran. Where could she go? Back to her tower? But they could easily corner her there. She found one of the sharply set stairs and scrambled up it, knowing she fled from death.

That the Voice controlled Nornoch there was no doubt. What did it matter now that she had learned how easily the Lurla could be fed? She would never have any chance to tell what she had learned, save to ears rendered already deaf to any words of hers.

Gasping, she reached the roof of the wall, ran along it. Now the sky was dark; she saw lightning split the clouds over the island's crown. It was as if the booming of the Voice had drawn the storm faster.

The Lurla—they must be alerted, sent to their posts! But if she were hunted, if the other wearers had laid aside their Eyes—

If she could find a hiding place then she could try to do her duty. The tower ahead was D'Huna's—her own was a turn of the wall away. She looked back once and saw the first guard come into the open.

Around the tower, on the outer edge—resolutely she kept her eyes from the rocks so far below. She had pushed up the Eye band to her shoulder for safekeeping so she could use her two hands to steady her. Step, step, do not think of the pursuers, keep her mind on making this perilous advance.

Again a flatter surface, which looked as wide and open as a road after that narrow detour. She flashed along it as the winds from the sea grew stronger. If the gale became worse she dared not try that outer passage at the other towers too often. The gusts could pluck her forth and dash her to her death below.

Even through the murk of the storm she could see her goal, though whether she had the courage and strength to reach it she did not know. A lesser spur of the rock, like that which supported the Voice, yet not so tall, was within leaping distance from the top of the wall at that point. As she well knew, that had a crevice halfway down its surface on the sea side wherein she could hide.

She reached the take-off point, measured the distance. If she faltered now she could never again summon up the needed spurt to make it. Recklessly she leaped for the spur, landing hard with a force that bruised her badly. But enough need for self preservation was left to make her crawl down into the break, wedging her body in as soon as she could force entrance.

The smell of the sea arose from below, but she was perched in a cramped space. The winds and waves were beginning their assault. She put on the Eye band, concentrated on the Lurla.

They—they were already at work! And at such a pace as her own prodding could never have won from them. Then this must be the effect of the Voice! No wonder D'Fani had felt safe, had allowed the wearers to be without their Eyes.

But—her mental picture steadied. The Lurla were working, yes, but without proper direction. They spun their congealing exudation along the walls, but also on the floors. And they were spinning too fast. Even as she contacted them, one went utterly limp and fell to the floor where another crawled unheedingly over it, encasing it with the hardening substance.

Frantically D'Eyree tried to slow them, give them direction as she had always done. To no avail. Whatever influence the Eyes had once had was gone, wiped out by the Voice. D'Fani was killing the Lurla, and there was nothing she could do—

D'Eyree was startled out of her concentration as something clanged against the rock near her head clattered down past her perch. A harpoon— She looked up, caught a glimpse of a guard taking fresh aim with another weapon. Cringing, she tried to make herself smaller.

But before the shot came, she heard a hoarse cry from above. Then, past the outer edge of the cleft in which she sheltered, a body plunged out and down. The force of the wind, or some misstep, had torn the guard from his post.

Before a second gained the same advantage she must be on the move, though she had to force herself to leave that illusion of safety to descend farther. So going she passed another hole, but it was too small to hold her. Three quarters of the way down she found what she sought, pulling herself into a deeper opening. She was certain now that she could not be sighted from overhead. That she could retreat any farther was impossible, as the sea was there, washing with vicious slaps among the rocks.

Once more she sought the Lurla. And her visual impression was so frightening that she was shocked. The expenditure of the sealing exudation was unbelievable. It ran in streams on the floor, dripped, before it could solidify, from the walls. In fact it now appeared to have some quality that kept it from that instant hardening which had been their aid.

Through the spur of rock that sheltered her she could still

feel the beat of the Voice, though most of the sound was now deadened by the sea. Was it that which worked upon the Lurla? And did D'Fani know—or care?

Duty urged her to climb again, to cry out to the people what was happening. But it would be to deaf ears, and she would doubtless be killed long before she reached any point from which they could hear her. She sat with the Eye band between her hands and tried to think.

The Eyes— The wearers were sensitive to the Eyes. If she could reach the mind of one of them, or more than one, with her warning—even though they had taken off their bands. She could only try. Earlier she had traced the old ways of communication with the sea, an exploit she had never thought to try before. Why not attempt this other thing? If she put all her strength to it—

She slipped the band from her arm, and as she did so it rapped sharply against the rock. To her horror one of the Eyes loosened, dropped. Before she could grab it, it rolled into a crevice and was gone. Only one left. But she could try, even though any power she might call upon was now halved.

D'Eyree concentrated as she never had before in her whole life, closing her eyes to better summon to mind the faces of the wearers. But she could not hold more than three at a time. Very well then—three— And to them, as if she stood before them, she cried aloud her warning, over and over, with no way of knowing either success or failure. At last she tired, tired so that she could not hold those faces in mind. Wearily she opened her eyes—upon darkness!

The storm— The sound of the sea was only a faint murmur. But she was in the dark! She put forth her hand and felt a wet, slimy surface.

Frantic, D'Eyree beat upon that surface. At first it seemed to her that it gave a little, but that was only illusion. As she ran her fingers across it, she realized the truth; she was walled in. And the smell of the stuff was fetid. It was Lurla slime.

That hole past which she had descended must have direct connection with the wall burrows, and some of that overflow had cascaded through it to cover her refuge's entrance. She was eternally trapped!

The horror of it made her sick. With the band at her breast she rocked back and forth, crying aloud. Entombed—alive—no escape— This was death—death—

Not death—not death—that stranger in her mind was awakening, taking over. Out—get out—not death—get out! But it was not D'Eyree who thought so—it was—

The clamor of the sea—she could breathe—she was out! And in her hands—

Ziantha sat up dazedly looking down at what she held. In one hand was the focus-stone, in the other a circle of shining metal with two settings in it—one held the twin to the stone, the other was empty! D'Eyree's Eyes!

But how—she looked along her body, half expecting to see the scaled skin, the alien form. No, she was in Vintra's body. And she—somehow she had not only found the twin stone, but had apported it from the past. But how long had she been in Nornoch? Turan—was he dead?

Lurching to her feet, she started back to the flyer. The sun was no longer high—instead it was nearly setting, sending a brilliant path across the waves. And the island was a dark and awesome blot. Ziantha shuddered away from the memory of those last moments before she had been able to tear away from D'Eyree. Never could she face that again. She must have won her freedom the very moment that the other had died. And if she had not—

Turan!

She tore open the cabin door to look within. He lay in his seat, his eyes closed. He looked dead.

"Turan!" She caught him by the shoulders, exerted her strength to draw him up, to make him open his eyes and see her.

13

Ziantha leaned over him, so filled with fear she could not immediately use mind-search to explore for any spark of life in Turan's body. But slowly those eyes opened; she saw them focus upon her, know her—

"Not dead." His slack lips tightened to shape the words. "You—got—out—"

"You knew that I was dying—back there?"

He did not seem to have even strength left to nod, but she could read his faint assent. Then she knew in turn—

"You helped me!"

"Trapped—needed—" His voice trailed away. Those eyes closed again, and his head rolled limply on his shoulders.

"No! Not now, Turan—we have won! See!" Before his closed eyes she held the two stones, one free, one in its setting. But perhaps it was too late, or was it?

She thought of the way D'Eyree had used the Eyes. Could she do likewise now? Could she give to Turan through them some of her own life force?

She tried to fit the band on her head, but its shape was too different. It had been fashioned for another species. At length she cupped the stones in her hands, held them to her forehead, and thought—thought life, energy, being, into Turan, seeking that spark almost driven out by death. And in that seeking she found it, united with it, fed it with her will, her belief, and confidence. As D'Eyree had driven the

154

Lurla, so did she now in fact drive Turan, feeding him all she had to give.

He stirred. Once more his eyes opened; he pulled himself up in the seat.

"No." His voice was stronger. "I can hold, but do not exhaust what you have to give. The time is not yet when it may be that all you can offer will be needed. We must get back— back to the beginning—Turan's tomb. And you must pilot this flyer."

Ziantha could not protest. In her mind he had earlier set the proper information. But in what direction? Where would she find a guide?

He might have picked that question out of her mind as he answered:

"I have set it—" Once more he lapsed into that state of nonbeing, hoarding his energy, she knew. Now it was her doing, all of it.

Ziantha pushed into the seat, fronted the controls. His instructions were clear in her mind. One did this and this. But could she lift the flyer off this stretch of rock, or would it crash into the sea, taking them both to a swift ending? There was no way to make sure but to try.

Her hands shaking a little, she brought the motor to life; the flyer moved forward. Now one did this and this. Frantically she worked at the controls, nor could she believe that she had succeeded until they were indeed airborne, climbing into the dusk of evening. She circled the rock that was all that was left of Nornoch, her eyes on the direction dial. The needle swung, steadied, and held. If he had been right that would take them back.

As they winged over the sea she tried to plan. That she had brought the second stone out of the past was still difficult for her to believe, unless the drawing power of its twin already in her hands and in use had been the deciding factor. But she was convinced that without careful study, her contemporaries would not be able to understand the psychic power locked in these gems.

The stones had been ancient in Nornoch, put to psychic uses by generations of sensitives. This in turn had built up in them reserves of energy. Rewakened by her use, that power had, in a manner, exploded. Would it now be as quickly dispersed, or could she harness it to return them to their own time?

Night came and still the flyer was airborne; the needle on the guide held steady. Turan moved once or twice, sighed. But she had not tried to reach him either by speech or mindsend. He was not to be disturbed. He needed all the strength he had to hold on. That he had given her of his last reserves in that moment of D'Eyree's death was a debt she must repay.

It was in the first dawn that she saw the coast lights, and, with those, lights moving in the sky as well, marking at least two other flyers. She could not maneuver this machine off course, nor did she know any way of defending it. She could only hope—

Locked on course, the flyer held steady, and she did not have to constantly monitor the controls. Now Ziantha drew from the breast of her robe the band of the Eyes and the loose gem. If she were taken, she must do all she could to keep the focus-stones. She set herself to pry the second of them from the band. A girdle clasp proved to be a useful tool for this, and a few minutes later she had it out.

The other flyers were boxing them in now, one on either side. Ziantha tensed. How soon would they fire upon them? Vintra's memory could not supply her with information. The rebels did not have many flyers, and Vintra had not used one. Would it be better to try to land? One glance at Turan told her of the impossibility of trying to cross country on foot.

Before her on the instrument board a light flashed on and

off in a pattern of several colors. Code—but one she could not read, much less answer. They were helpless until the flyer reached the goal Turan had set.

When no attack came, Ziantha breathed a little easier. Zuha had ordered them shot down on sight, but that had not happened. Therefore it might be that other orders had been issued since. How long had they been on the island? She did not know whether it was only part of a day or much longer.

The flyer bored steadily on into the morning. Ziantha was very hungry, thirsty, and her sensitive's control could no longer banish those needs. She found a compartment in which emergency rations were carried. The contents of the tube were not appetizing but she gulped them down. Turan? She drew forth a second tube, prepared to uncap it.

"No." His word was hardly more than a whisper. He was looking beyond her to the flyer that was their escort—or guard.

"They have not attacked," she told him the obvious. "For a while they tried to communicate by code. Now they do nothing."

"The focus-stones—" He made such a visible effort to get out those words that her anxiety grew.

"Here," she held out her hand so he could see them lying on her palm.

"Must keep—"

"I know." She had not yet thought of a hiding place. If they were taken, she, at least, would be searched. She had no doubt of that. She ran one hand through her hair. Its thick sweep was a temptation, but there was no safe way of anchoring them in those locks. There remained her mouth. Experimentally she fitted the stones, one within each cheek. They were about the same size as the pits of dried umpa fruit, and she believed she could carry them so.

With them so close, she could draw upon their energy.

Somehow, as her tongue moved back and forth touching first one and then the other, Ziantha felt a little cheered. They had had such amazing good fortune in their quest so far; they were still free, with both stones. Yet, she knew that there was danger in any building of confidence. And no sane person depended upon fortune to last.

There was a faint beeping sound from the controls. She had set the flyer on maximum speed when they had left the island, recklessly intent only on reaching their goal as quickly as possible. What fueled the machine she did not know, pushing away that worry when she had so much else to concern her. Was this a signal that that energy was failing them?

But it was the guide dial that made that sound. They must be near to the tomb. Where could she land—and how?

The flyer shook, broke out of its forward sweep. Ziantha caught at the controls. But they were locked against her attempt to free them!

"Turan!"

He turned his head with painful effort.

"They have us—in—a—traction pull—" he whispered.

A pull that was taking them earthward. They would crash! She sat with her hands on those useless controls and sent out mind-seek. The in-and-out reception of alien thought was blighting, but that they were captive she understood. And they were being brought down to their captor's desire almost within sight of their goal.

"They—want—us—secretly—" Turan was rousing, pulling himself higher in the seat. "No one to know what happens—"

Ziantha probed, fought to reach and hold one of those mind waves. Perhaps it was the Eyes that gave her the skill to seize and hold.

Zuha!

The thoughts were blurred. It was like hearing only a few words of a whispered conversation. But the girl learned something. Yes, Turan was right; they were being brought in for a

158

landing at a small private field, away from Singakok. Zuha wanted no interference while she dealt with them. Had they been of her own world and time, Ziantha could have used the power to control, to alter their memories for long enough to escape.

"Ride with them—not—against," Turan said. "Zuha wants us dead."

Ziantha caught his suggestion. Could they use the hate and fear of the alien woman to take them where they must go? Could she feed Zuha's desires?

"I shall be dead," Turan answered her chain of thought. "You must project to the High Consort a great fear of your own—one she will understand."

"The fear of being once more buried with you," Ziantha agreed. But it would be true, painfully true. All the horror she had known as D'Eyree entombed in that sealed crevice flooded back to make her sick. Could she face such an ordeal again? For it might well prove to be the truth, that, returned to Turan's tomb, they would remain there.

"There is no other way. Our door lies there."

Of course she had always known that in the back of her mind, but she had pushed it from her, refusing to face it squarely. This was the pattern they must follow to the end. Once again the tomb and the hope of return through it.

"I am dead," he said. "Your fear must be fed to her. In this I cannot help you."

"I know."

With the same concentration she had used to learn the method for that invasion of Jucundus's apartment which had begun this whole mad foray, Ziantha began to build her one chance. The irregular wave length meant that Zuha would not have clear reception. And so she could not be sure she had succeeded until some action of the other revealed it.

But she summoned fear, which was easy to do, fear of the dark, of imprisonment in that dark, of death, though she dared not allow panic to disrupt the careful marshaling of thought. Not that—not the tomb again! To die entombed beside the dead. Not that! She built up the strength of her broadcast in vivid mind pictures. Ziantha was shivering now, her hands locked about the useless controls.

The flyer was spiraling down. She saw trees rising to meet them, wondered for a moment if they would crash. But no, Zuha wanted more than any quick death, she wanted vengeance on Turan, and more on the woman she believed responsible for Turan's return. Feed her the thought of death in the tomb. Ziantha held to her mind-send as the flyer bounced along the rough ground.

Turan had been shaken against her in that landing. His body was an inert weight. To her eyes he was dead. Dare she test now? No, she must continue to concentrate on that suggestion—the return of the dead—and the living—to the tomb.

She made no move to escape from the flyer. Let them believe she was cowering here in fear. And they would not be far wrong. The dark passion she had touched in Zuha's mind was enough to promise the worst. But, if only the High Consort believed the worst to be what Ziantha tried to suggest to her!

The door was wrenched open with force, and she saw the face of an armsman. He stared at her, at Turan lying limply against her shoulder; then he was ordered aside by an officer.

"Lord Commander!" The man caught at Turan to draw him away from the girl. The body sprawled forward in his grasp. With an exclamation, the officer involuntarily jerked back, Turan falling, to dangle head and shoulders over the edge of the door.

"Dead!" the officer cried out. "The Lord Commander is dead!"

"As he has been!" There was triumph in the High Consort's reply. "There was only the sorcery of this witch to keep him seemingly alive. But he has eluded her at last." She stood wrapped in a heavy cloak against the snow-laden wind, her eyes hot as she looked beyond the body to Ziantha. Now she leaned forward, her pose almost reptilian as she hissed:

"He is safely dead. But you still live, witch! And now you are under my hand."

The armsman and the officer had drawn Turan's body out of the flyer, laid it upon the ground. Ziantha did not move; only with her last spurt of mind-send she tried to reach, to implant in the High Consort what must be done.

"Your Grace," the officer looked up from where he knelt by Turan, "what are your orders?"

"What should they be—that my lord be returned to his place of rest where we laid him in honor and respect. And let this be done without further delay before such witnesses as will bear the proper news to the people and put an end to this wild tale of returns and miracles. Let the Priest-Lord of Vut be summoned to reseal the spirit door with Vut's own seal, which no witchery can break."

She spoke swiftly as one who had planned for this moment and intended to see her orders carried out with all dispatch. Turan, dead, must vanish again, and as speedily as possible. But was he dead? Ziantha could only hope that the spark of that other still clung to life so he could win out in the end.

"And the witch, Your Grace?" The officer arose to his feet, came over to the cabin to draw her forth.

"Ah, yes, the witch. Bring her forth!"

The grasp upon her hurt as he pulled her out roughly. She hoped that her concealment of the Eyes would serve. The armsman twisted her arms behind her back, holding her so to face Zuha.

"The priests would have you," the High Consort said slowly, "to tear forth the secret of your witchery. But priests are men before their vows are taken. I would blast you with the flamer where you stand, save that that is too quick a death. You have companied with my lord and brought him back to life—for your purposes. What purposes?"

"Ask of him," Ziantha said. "I moved by his will, not by my own."

Her head rocked from the blow Zuha struck with lightning speed then. Ziantha feared the most that she might have revealed the presences of the Eyes, for the inside of her mouth was cut by the edges of one of the stones.

But as she stood, dazed a little from the force and pain of that blow, the High Consort stepped back a pace.

"It does not matter. Whatever he, or you, attempted has failed. Turan is dead and will go to the tomb. As for you—"

Ziantha braced herself. This was the crucial moment. Would her attempts to influence Zuha succeed?

"Since my lord saw fit, as you tell me, to use you, then it would seem he found you well suited for his tomb service. Thus you shall return with him. Only this time there shall be no escape, through the spirit door or otherwise! There shall be measures taken to make sure of that, above all else do I swear it so!"

She turned to the officer. "You will take charge of my lord's body and bear it to the lodge. I shall send those to prepare him for sleep, which this time will not be disturbed. You will take this witch also, and her you will keep under strict guard until the time comes that she also be returned whence she came. And your life will answer for hers."

"So be it, Your Grace."

Ziantha was so full of relief, for that moment, that she was hardly aware of the rough handling that stowed her into one of the ground cars, brought her forth again at a building among trees. She was bound and dumped on the floor of a room, left under the eyes of two armsmen who watched her with such an intensity of concentration that it was clear they thought she might disappear before their very eyes.

Lying there, her first relief ebbed as she considered the ordeal before her. Even though she had escaped D'Eyree's death, she was not certain she could make the second transfer to her own time. She had drawn so heavily on her powers, that even with the Eyes she could not be sure she had enough energy left. And she would also have the need to draw "Turan" with her.

Rest was what she needed. And in spite of her present discomfort of body, she set herself to relaxing by sensitive techniques, withdrawing into the inner part of herself to renew and store all the force she could generate.

Ziantha submerged herself now in memory, summoning to mind each detail of that plundered outer room of the tomb. If she was to have a point to focus upon it must be that. Her last memory of it had been when she was in the hands of the Jack captain, being forced to gaze into the focus-stone. But she pushed aside her mind-picture of that action, concentrated instead upon the chamber itself—the walls, the crumbling debris of what long ago thieves had smashed. Bit by bit she built up her mental picture of it as she had seen it the moment they had broken their way in.

She rejected any portion that seemed uncertain, for the reality of that chamber must exist, must *be* so she could center her will and power on returning to it. And that her memory was faulty, too broken by the actions of others for accurate anchorage, she was well aware. Again, until the testing, she could never count on success.

Having made her mind-chamber as clear and precise as she could, she allowed it to slip into memory again. Turan— she wished she dared to arouse him. But perhaps the slight effort of receiving a mind-send might shake his hold—if he was not already gone. No, this was her own battle, and she must not count on any help at hand except from her own strength and knowledge.

She had done what she could in preparation. Now let her

once more sink into that half-tranced state of mind which would allow her to conserve her strength—wait— Deliberately she forced away all thought of the next hour—the next moment. Her breathing was shallow, even, her eyes closed. She might have been asleep, save that this state was no sleep of body.

Ziantha visualized her own form of peace and contentment. There was a pool of silent, fragrant water, and on it her body floated free. Above her only the arch of the sky. She was as light as a leaf on the surface of the pool. She was as free as the sky—

The sound of a voice broke the bubble of her peace in a painful shattering. It came so suddenly she did not understand the meaning of the words. But there were hands on her, jerking her upright with unnecessary roughness. As she opened her eyes she saw the officer in the doorway. So it was time.

They dumped her without ceremony in the back of a car, where she was bumped and rolled back and forth by the motion of their going. She could not see out, and she made no effort to tap the minds of those with her. Turan was not here. Doubtless they transported him with more dignity.

The drive seemed long, and she was badly bruised—half dazed—but in time the vehicle came to a stop, and she was pulled out. This place she knew. They were at the foot of that rise down which she and Turan had made such an awkward descent on the night of their escape. It was not night now but late afternoon, and the details of earth, rock, and vegetation were clear.

Her two guards kept her upright to one side, away from the cortege climbing the hill to the spirit door. There was a priest of Vut, of the highest rank, Vintra's memory told her. He intoned a chant as he went, supported by two lesser prelates, one carrying a heavy mallet, the other a box, while the Priest-Lord of Vut scattered on the wind handsful of ashy powder.

Turan, borne on a bier supported by two officers, followed. Except for his face, he had been covered with a long, richly embroidered drapery, over-worked in metallic threads with designs sacred to Vut. Behind came three armsmen and then the High Consort in her robe of yellow mourning, but her veil was thrown well back as if she wished to see every detail of this recommitment of her lord to the earth she determined would hold him safely this time.

Ziantha shivered with more than the lash of the wind, the bite of the snow settling down around them. She watched the Priest-Lord of Vut lean over the bier, sift upon it more of the ashes. They must be standing by the open spirit door. Two of the armsmen lowered themselves through that door, ready to arrange the commander's body.

Then the bier was attached to ropes and slid through the opening to disappear from sight. When the armsmen reappeared, Zuha made a gesture to Ziantha's guards.

They were eager as they pulled and pushed her along. Now she struggled, cried out, for Zuha must not suspect that she greeted this end with other than the height of fear. The wind was harsh, icy as it met them full on at the top of the cliff.

"But we should know how she did this thing—" The Priest-Lord of Vut stood before Zuha, authority in his tone. "If the rebels have such powers—"

"If they have such powers, Reverence, will they not be able to use them to bend living men to their will as well? Did not the armsman we found at Xuth tell of how this one controlled him so when he would go to the Lord Commander's aid she rendered him unconscious? She is a danger to us all. Would you take her to the heart of Vut to practice her sorcery?"

The priest turned to look at Ziantha. Was he going to protest more? Here at the very last would he defeat all she had fought for?

"She seems safe enough a prisoner now, High Consort. Would she allow herself to be so taken if she had the great powers you fear?"

"She does not have the Lord Commander. In some way he aided her in this. I do not know how, but it is so; she even admitted it. I tell you such is a danger as have not seen before. There is only one thing she fears—look well at her now. She fears return to the tomb. Seal it with the seal of Vut and she will trouble us no more!"

For a moment or two he hesitated. The armsmen and the officers had closed ranks behind Zuha, and it was apparent he decided not to stand against them.

Zuha knew that she had won. She swung around to fully face Ziantha and her guards.

"Strip the witch!" she ordered crisply. "If she has aught which seems a thing of power, let it be given to the Priest-Lord. Let her take nothing but her bare skin this time!"

They ripped her clothing from her, and then one of the officers caught her by the shoulders, pushed her forward. She felt them run a rope about her arms. Half frozen in the lash of the wind, she was dropped over, lowered. A moment later all light vanished as they clapped down the spirit door.

14

Ziantha could hear a dull pounding overhead as she lay there in the freezing dark. They were making very sure that the spirit door was sealed, that Turan would not return again. Turan— She used mind-search—meeting nothing!

He was gone. Dead? She was alone in this place of horror, and if she escaped it would only be through her own efforts.

Ziantha spat the gems out in her hands, pressed them against her forehead as D'Eyree had done to achieve the greatest power.

She was not Vintra left to die in the dark—she was Ziantha! Ziantha! Fiercely she poured all her force of will into that identification. Ziantha!

A whirling, a sense of being utterly alone, lost. With it a fear of this nothingness, of being forever caught and held in a place where there was no life at all. Ziantha—she was *Ziantha!* She had identity, this was *so!*

Ziantha! Her name cried out, offering an anchorage.

In this place which was nothingness she tried to use it as a guide.

Ziantha!

She opened her eyes. Her weakness was such that she would have fallen had she not been held on her feet. Iuban.

"She is coming out of it," he spoke over her shoulder to someone the girl could not see. But the relief of knowing that she had made the last transfer successfully was so great she wilted into unconsciousness.

Noise—shouting, a cry broken off by a scream of agony. Unwillingly she was being drawn back to awareness once again. She was lying in the dust, as if Iuban had dropped or thrown her from him. There was no light except that which came with the crackle of laser beams well over her head. Dazed, she pressed against the wall wishing she could burrow into its substance, free herself from this scene of battle.

Ziantha? Mind call—from Turan? No. Turan was dead, this was— Her mind was slow, so exhausted that it fumbled, this was Ogan! She had a flash of reassurance at being able to fit a name to that seeking.

The firing had stopped and now a bright beam of light dazzled her eyes as it swept to illumine the looted tomb. She saw a huddled body, recognized one of the crewmen who had brought her here.

Someone bent over her. She saw Ogan, put out a hand weakly.

"Come!" he swept her up, carried her out of that black and haunted place into the open where the freshness of the air she drew in was a promise of safety ahead. But she was so tired, so drained. Her head lay heavy on Ogan's shoulder as the darkness closed about her once more.

How long did she sleep? It had been night, now it was day. For she did not wake in the ship but out in the open, with a sunlit sky arching above her. And, for the first moments of that awakening, Ziantha was content to know she was free, safely returned to her own time. But that other—he had not returned!

The sense of loss that accompanied that realization was suddenly a burden to darken the sky, turning all her triumph into defeat. She sat up in a bedroll, though that movement brought dizziness to follow.

No ship—then— But where—and how? There were peaks of rock like shattered walls, and, in a cup among those, bedrolls. Ogan sat cross-legged on one such within touching dis-

168

tance, watching her in a contemplative way. Before him on the ground was a piece of cloth and resting on that—the Eyes!

Ziantha shuddered. Those she never wanted to see again.

"But you must!" Ogan's thought ordered.

"Why?" She asked aloud.

"There are reasons. We shall discuss them later." He picked up one end of that cloth, dropped it to cover the gems. "But first—" He arose and went to fetch her an E-ration tube.

There were two other men in the camp, and they were, she noted, plainly, on sentry duty, facing outward on opposite sides of the cup, weapons in hand. Ogan expected attack. But where was Yasa? The Salarika had expected Ogan to join forces with her. Had Iuban made Yasa a prisoner?

"Where is Yasa?" Ziantha finished the ration, felt its renewing energy spread through her.

Ogan reseated himself on the bedroll. In this rugged setting he looked out of place, overshadowed by the grim rocks—almost helpless. But Ziantha did not make the mistake of believing that.

He did not answer her at once, and he had a mind-shield up. Was—was Yasa dead? So much had changed in her life that Ziantha could even believe the formidable veep might have been removed from it. Iuban had tried to use her powers to his own advantage. She struggled now to remember what she had heard before he had forced her to look into the focus-stone. It was plain he had been moving against Yasa, even as the Salarika had earlier schemed to take over the expedition herself.

"Yasa"—Ogan broke through her jumbled thought—"is on the Jack ship. I believe that they intend to use her as a hostage—or bargaining point."

"With you—for them?" Ziantha gestured to the covered stones.

"With me—for you and them," he assented. "Unfortunately

169

for them I have all the necessities, and I do not need Yasa. In fact I much prefer not having to deal with her."

"But Yasa—she expected you to come, to help—"

"Oh, I had every intention of coming, and, as you see, I did. To your service I did. Yasa may be all powerful on Korwar, but here she has stretched her authority far too thin. I am afraid it has just snapped in her face."

"But—" Ogan had always been Yasa's man, a part of her establishment. Ziantha had believed him so thoroughly loyal to the veep that his attachment could not be questioned.

"You find it difficult to believe that I have plunged into a foray on my own? But this is a matter which touches *my* talents. Such a discovery is not to be left to those who do not understand the power of what has been uncovered. They cannot use it properly; therefore, why should they have it to play with in their bungling fashion? I *know* what it is, they only suspect as yet."

He knew what it was, Ziantha digested that. And he knew she had used it. He would take her in turn, use her, wring her dry of all she had learned. Make her— A small spark of rebellion flared deep in Ziantha. She was not going to serve Ogan's purposes so easily.

And with that determined, she began to think more clearly. That other sensitive—it had not been Ogan who had entered Turan and shared her adventures. But the sensitive had worked with Harath and— Was he someone Ogan had brought in? If so, why had the parapsychologist not mentioned him?

Ziantha realized that there was more than a little mystery left and the sooner she learned all she could, the better. At that moment she felt Ogan's testing probe and snapped down a mind-barrier.

Trace of a frown on his face. The probe grew stronger. She stared back at him level-eyed. Then, for the first time in her relationship with him, she made resistance plain.

"Ask your questions if you wish—aloud."

His probe was withdrawn. "You are a foolish child. Do you think because you have managed to use the stones, after some undisciplined fashion, you are now my equal? That is pure nonsense; your own intelligence should tell you so."

"I do not claim to be anything more than I am." From somewhere came the words and even as she uttered them Ziantha knew wonder at her defiance. Had she indeed changed? She knew well all that Ogan could do to her mentally and physically to gain his own will. Still there was that in her now which defied him to try it—a new confidence. Though until she was more certain of what she had gained she must be wary.

"That is well." He seemed satisfied, though her statement might be considered an ambiguous one. He must be judging her by what she had been and not what she now was.

"Where is Harath?" she asked abruptly, wishing to clear up the mystery of who had been with her, yet not wanting to ask openly.

"Harath?" He looked at her sharply.

She held tight to her barrier. Had she made an error in asking that?

But Harath had been here; she had known his touch, that she could not have mistaken. Why then should Ogan be surprised that she asked for him? Harath was Ogan's tool; it was natural that they be together, just as it had been natural for the unknown sensitive to use the alien to contact her.

"Harath is on Korwar."

Ziantha was startled by so flat a lie. Why did Ogan think she would believe it? He knew that Harath had been used to contact her; there was no reason to conceal it. And if he denied Harath so, then what of the other sensitive? Was this loss of one who had been a tool such that Ogan must cover with lies? But lies which he knew she would not accept? She felt for an instant or two as if she were plunged back into that whirling place which had no sane anchorage. Ogan was not acting in character, unless he had devised some kind of a test she did not understand.

Another thrust of mind-probe, one forceful enough to have penetrated her defenses in other days. But she held against it. Until she knew more she must hold her barrier.

"Why do you expect to find Harath here?" If his defeat at reading her thoughts baffled him, his chagrin was not betrayed by his tone.

"Why should I not?" Ziantha countered. "Have we not always used him for relaying and intensifying the power? Here do we not need him most?"

To Ziantha, her logic sounded good. But would Ogan accept it? And where was Harath? Why had Ogan made such a mystery of his presence?

Ogan arose. "Harath is too unique to risk," he said. His head turned from her; he stood as if listening. Then, in some haste, he crossed the depression to join one of the sentries.

Ziantha watched him. It was plain he expected trouble. It might be that Iuban had grown impatient, or even that Yasa had once more made common cause with the Jack captain when she discovered Ogan a traitor. The Salarika was no fool. Though she had made an independent bid for what the focus-stone might deliver, she would never have shut off all roads of retreat.

The Eyes—Ziantha's attention shifted to the stones under their cloth covering. That they were a prize beyond any one tomb, no matter how rich, she now realized. Ogan suspected that, and perhaps Yasa also. But they did not have her proof. There was also this: were the Eyes unique in answering to one sensitive alone, or could any, including Ogan, bring them into action?

She had worn them twice in those other worlds, as Vintra, who had not known the power of the stone that was forced upon her by her enemies, and as D'Eyree, who had known

172

it very well and had put it to use. She had not been an on-looker, but had entered into Vintra, D'Eyree. Therefore the stones had answered her will. Were they "conditioned" then to her? And if so, did she now have a bargaining point with Ogan?

But that other kept intruding into her half-plans and hopes. Who was the sensitive who had been sacrificed to help her out of the past—and where was Harath, that source of energy? Ziantha tried not to think of Turan, except as a problem she must solve for her own safety in future relations with Ogan. She tried to hold off the dark shadow that came at the very name of Turan. Turan was a dead man—and he who had accompanied her through that wild adventure had been a stranger, some tool of Ogan's, to whom she owed nothing now. But she did! The fact that Ogan had used him made him no less. Ogan had used her, too, in the past, over and over again, molded and trained her to do just what he—or Yasa—wanted. So why could she feel that this other was any less than she had been? Ogan had used him and he had died. Ogan would try again to use her, and, if the circumstances answered, he would discard her as easily at any moment.

Ziantha snatched up the stones, put them in the front of her planet suit, resealing it. If Ogan thought to treat her so, he might have a surprise. She knew what D'Eyree had been able to do with the Eyes. It might be that she could put them to far more potent use than Ogan guessed. And that she would try it before the end of this venture, Ziantha was now certain.

There remained Harath. If the alien were still on-planet she would reach him. The bond between them was one which Ogan had first brought into being, that was true. However she wanted to hold that much of the past. Of all who were now on the surface of this half-destroyed world, Harath was the only one whom she could trust.

Ogan came back to her. "We are moving on."

"To your ship?" She hoped not, not yet. Oddly enough while she was in the open she at least had the illusion of freedom.

"Not yet." But he did not amplify that, as he knelt to fasten her bedroll.

With those slung as packs, and the men each carrying in addition a sling of supplies, they edged between the fanglike rocks and climbed down into a very deep valley. In the depths of this a thread of water trickled along, and there were some stunted bushes. Here and there a coarse tuft of grass gave more signs of life than she had seen elsewhere.

What had happened to the world of Turan to reduce Singakok and the land around it to this state? Only a disastrous conflict or some unheard-of natural catastrophe would have wrought this. And how many planet centuries ago had it all happened?

The footing was very rough and, though Ogan apparently wanted to set a fast pace, they did not keep to what was any better than perhaps a slow walk on smoother surface. Also the scrambling up and down was most wearying, and Ogan himself began to breathe heavily, rest more often.

As they traveled, the valley opened out, the vegetation grew in greater luxuriance, though all of it was stunted, rising at the highest no farther than one's shoulder. Yet as it thickened it slowed their advance even more. So far Ziantha had seen no other life except that rooted in the soil. And she wondered if all else had been slaughtered in the doom which came to Singakok.

Then one of the men gave a furious exclamation and flashed a laser beam into the bushes. As he called a warning Ziantha saw on his out-thrust boot the scoring of teeth spattered with yellow foam.

"Lizard thing—watch out for it." He set his foot on a rock and leaned over to examine the boot. "Didn't go through."

174

Then he dabbled his foot in the stream, letting the current wash away that foam. Meanwhile his partner methodically lasered the ground ahead, cleaning it down to the bare rock, until Ogan caught at his arm.

"Do not use all your charge on this—"

The man jerked away. "I am not going to get a poison bite," he returned sullenly. But he did not continue with the laser.

Their progress slowed again beyond that clearer section because they had to watch the ground carefully. Ziantha's legs ached. She was not used to such vigorous and continued exercise, and she liked this ground less with every moment they fought their way across it.

Twice Ogan had fallen back a pace or so behind; then they made one of their frequent halts, his attitude still that of one who listened. Ziantha decided he must be using mind-send to check on some possible pursuer. But she did not release her own probe to follow his. It might be a trick of Ogan's to force her barrier down to his own advantage. She must be on constant guard with him, as she well knew.

They came to a barrier formed by the land. The stream spilled here in a long ribbon of falling water over the edge of a drop. And they must now strike east, climbing up one of the valley walls, since the descent before them was too steep to attempt.

This left them in the open on fairly level ground, and the attitude of both Ogan and his men was that of those exposed to possible attack. So they hurried on, Ogan even taking her by the arm and pulling her forward, coming thus to another upstand of rocks into which they crawled.

Here they broke out rations and ate. Ziantha rubbed her aching legs. She was not sure if she could keep going, though she was very certain Ogan would see to it that she did if they had to drag her. It was plain he wanted to avoid some pursuers. Iuban was perhaps not waiting for negotiations over Yasa but again striking out on his own as he had when he took her to the tomb.

"Is it Iuban?" She rolled the empty E-tube into a tight ball.

Ogan merely grunted. She recognized the signs of ultraconcentration. He was trying mind-search, striving to learn what he could. But there was no confidence in his tension; rather the strain of his effort grew more apparent. And she was troubled by that. In the ordinary way any crewman such as Iuban led would be well open to reading by a master as competent as Ogan. That the mysterious pursuers were not, as his concern suggested, meant they were equipped with shields. But why, if he had discovered that fact, as he would have at once, did he still struggle to touch?

And why had he not ordered her to back him in a thrust? It was, Ziantha decided, as if he had a reason to keep her from learning the nature of what he sought to penetrate. Or was she only imagining things? She leaned her back against an upstanding rock and closed her eyes.

If Ogan was not present she could try herself. Not to cast to what might be trailing them, but for Harath. Somehow it was important that she find out where the alien had gone and why Ogan denied he was here.

And for Harath—again her thoughts slid on to the one whose power Harath had guided to her: Ogan's tool—Turan —but he was not Turan. She tried to recall now all those she had seen from time to time visiting Ogan's lab at the villa. He could have been any one of those, for Ogan had kept her aloof from the others he used in his experiments. The one thing that puzzled her now was that Turan (he must remain Turan for she knew no other name to call him) was indeed a trained sensitive of such power that she could not easily see him subordinated to Ogan.

He was not one to be used as a tool, but rather one who used tools himself. The physical envelope he had worn as Turan continued to mislead her. Now she strove to build up a personality with no association with the dead Lord Commander. It was like fitting together shards of some artifact of whose real shape she was unaware.

But that depression which she had held in abeyance settled down on her full force. In all her life, in the Dipple and after Yasa had taken her from that place of despair, she had had no one of her own. The Salarika veep had given her shelter, education, a livelihood. But Ziantha had always known that this was not because she was herself, but because she represented an investment that was expected to repay Yasa for her attentions many times over.

Ogan had been a figure of awe at first, then one to be feared and resented. She admitted his mastery, and she hated him—yes, she recognized her depth of emotion now—for it. Sooner or later now she would have to face Ogan and fight for her freedom. She had not been a real person when he had taught her, only a thing he could shape. Now she was herself, and she intended to remain so.

Yasa and Ogan—they had been the main factors in her existence. To neither was she bound by any ties of softer emotion. Harath—the closest she had ever come to having what one might deem a "friend"—was the queer alien creature. She trusted Harath.

Then—Turan. It had not been master and pupil between them, or benefactor and servant, but rather what she imagined was the comradeship between two crewmen, or two of the Patrol who faced a common danger and depended upon one another in times of crisis.

As he had depended upon her at the last!

Ziantha felt moisture gather under her closed eyelids. She had never wept except for physical reasons when a child—cold, hunger. These tears now were for a sense of loss transcending all those, a wound so deep within her that she was just beginning to know what damage it had wrought. And

Ogan had done this thing—sent the other after her—and had left him to die.

Therefore her reckoning with Ogan, overdue as it was, would be eagerly sought by her. But at her time, not his. For she did not in the least undervalue her opponent.

She was roused from her thoughts by Ogan's hand on her shoulder.

"Up—we have to get under cover. Mauth has been scouting ahead and has found shelter."

The girl glanced around. One of the men was gone, the other held a click com in his hand, was listening to the message it ticked out. She got to her feet with a sigh. If it were much further she was not sure she could make it.

"Hurry!" Ogan pulled at her.

Of course they had to climb again and took a very roundabout way, as if Ogan was determined they remain as much undercover as possible. Twice Ziantha slipped and fell, and the second time she was unable to regain her feet unaided. But Ogan drew her along, cursing under his breath.

So he brought her to a cave, and thrust her back into the shadows well away from the door. When she sprawled there again he made no move to help her up, but let her lay where she had fallen, while he returned to the entrance, giving a low-voiced order to the crewmen that sent one of them away once more.

15

Night shadows were gathering. The sun, so brazen and naked over this riven land, was gone, though its brilliant banners still lingered in part of the sky. Ziantha crouched at the back of the cave. Her body ached from the unaccustomed exercise, but her mind was alert.

The man Ogan had sent out did not return. Twice click signals she could not decode came, and with each Ogan grew more restless. Whatever his plans, they were manifestly being frustrated. At last he came back to where she sat, hunkered down so that their faces were on a level.

"You are safe here—"

"Safe from Iuban?" she dared to interrupt. "Are his men trailing us?"

"Iuban!" He gestured as if the Jack captain were a gaming piece of little value to be swept from the board. "No—there is a greater complication than that. There is a Patrol ship finned down out there!"

"Patrol! But how—" Among all the possible dangers she had not expected this one.

Ogan shrugged. "How indeed? But there are always ears to listen, mouths to be bought. Yasa went through Waystar. And Waystar is not Guild; it can be infiltrated—in fact it has been, at least once. And there is a chance I may have been followed also. But how they came does not matter. That they are here does."

He was silent for a moment, eying her narrowly.

"You know the penalty for using sensitive power for the Guild—remember it well, girl."

Her mouth was suddenly dry. Yes, it had been hammered into her from the earliest days of her training what her fate would be if the forces of the law caught her during a Guild foray. Not death, no. In some ways death would be more welcome. But erasure—brain erasure—so that the person who was Ziantha would vanish from life, and some dull-witted creature fit only for a routine task would stand in her place. All memory, personality, wiped permanently away.

There was a glint of satisfaction in Ogan's expression; he must have seen her recoil.

"Yes, remember that and keep remembering it, Ziantha. Erasure—" Ogan drawled that last word. It became an obscenity when one knew its meaning. "You stay undercover exactly as you are bid. Unfortunately the Patrol ship has finned down in just that area where it can cause us the greatest inconvenience, and we have to remain hidden until they convince themselves that the Jack ship is the only one here."

"But your ship—they can locate that."

He shook his head. "Not a ship, Ziantha. I landed from space in an L-B. And that is under detect protection. My ship will return, but it is not in orbit now to be picked up by a Patrol detect."

"They have other detects, persona ones, do they not? What if they use those?" She fought for control, determined not to let the fear he sparked in her become panic.

"Naturally. And they are out there now, combing with such. They will pick up the Jacks, unless they are equipped with distorts. We do have those—"

A distort could throw off a persona, she knew. Just as a visual distort could throw off sight. There was one other way —if they had a sensitive—

"They do not!" Ogan might have read her mind. "Though they might have on such a mission, by so much fortune we are favored. I have probed for one and there is no trace. So we are safe as long as we take precautions. But we do not have much time. The L-B is set on a time return, and unless I can get to it and reset it, it will take off without us."

"You are going to try that?"

"I must. Therefore I shall leave you here with Mauth. There is always the hope that the Patrol and the Jacks will keep each other busy. But understand—if they find you"—he again made that sweep-away gesture—"you are finished. There is no one to lift a hand to save you. So—you have the focus-stones—give them to me. I shall put them in the L-B for safety."

"They will be of no value to you." Ziantha began her own game. It all depended on how much she could make Ogan believe. "They are now mind-linked to me. I have learned their full secret, and they will answer only to the one who awakened them."

Would he accept that? He had no way of testing it one way or the other since his lab equipment was worlds away.

"What can you do with them?" he asked after a moment.

Ziantha thought frantically. She had to provide some major advantage now for keeping the stones.

"If the Patrol here has no sensitive, I may be able to use these as a mind distort. They were once used for control-ling—" For controlling the Lurla, animal things—would they work on men? But she need not explain that to Ogan.

"You have learned much. When there is time you shall tell me all of it."

"All," she echoed as if she were still under his domination.

"But perhaps it is best that you do keep the stones," Ogan continued to her great relief. "And you shall stay with Mauth until my return."

Ziantha knew that he went unwillingly, that above all he was now intrigued by her disclosures and frustrated that he could not put her statements to instant testing. Ogan had never been the most patient of men where his absorption in parapsychology was concerned.

The girl watched him make a wary exit from the cave. Why she had not gladly surrendered the stones to him she did not know, only that she could not. Just as she had brought what had been in D'Eyree's hands from one past, and both of them out of Vintra's time, so were they joined to her now.

She took them out, holding them in her clenched fist. If she ever looked into them again where would she be—Singakok? Nornoch? Neither did she want to see again.

Nor would she use them to serve Ogan. If the need to choose came she would see that they were lost somewhere in this wilderness of broken rocks, beyond his reach.

There remained Harath. Ogan must have left him at the L-B, though she still could not understand his denial that the alien was on-planet. With Ogan gone she could call—from Harath she could certainly learn the truth.

With the stones in her hands, Ziantha let down her mind barrier for the first time since Ogan had found her. She sent out a thought probe, the image of Harath bright and clear in her mind. Greatly daring she advanced the call farther and farther.

"Harath?"

His recognition was as sharp as her call. And then, before she could question him—

Warning, denial, a surge of need—do not try to communicate—use our touch as a guide.

Harath could not then be at the L-B; perhaps he had wandered away, searching for them. Or had he fled Ogan for some reason? But he would not answer. The thread between them was very faint and thin by his will, a guide but not a way of exchanging information. Save the fact that he held it so conveyed a warning.

She leaned her head forward so her chin rested on her knees as she thought of Harath, kept that thread intact. He was coming to her—there was danger—

A sharp clicking interrupted her thoughts. Her head jerked up and around. It was now dark in the cave. The guard at the mouth was only a blot against the slightly lighter sky. That must be his com in action.

"Gentle fem," his voice out of the gloom, using the customary address of everyday life, which seemed strange here, "a message from veep Ogan. We are to move out—to the east."

"He said—stay here." Move now when Harath was on the way? She must not.

"The plans are changed, gentle fem. The Jacks or the Patrol are closing in with some type of persona detect that is new."

Perhaps, she thought anxiously, they have picked up my call to Harath.

"Come on!" Mauth did not speak with any courtesy now. He was plainly prepared to carry out his instructions by force if need be.

Ziantha thought furiously. She had the stones with all the power they represented. This man was no sensitive, and this was her chance for escape. She must take it and wait for Harath.

"I am coming." But she did not stir from her place. Instead she broke that cord with Harath and bent all the energy she could summon into a projection aimed at Mauth.

"We go down—" He turned and scrambled out of the cave. Nor did he look back to see that she was not with him. Her attempt was successful, and to his mind she was beside him now.

Ziantha was honestly astounded at her success. Ogan could do this with those who had no talents. But that she could project a believable hallucination was new. Her confidence in the might of the stones grew.

But she could not hold this long. Which meant that with Mauth away from the cave she must leave also. As soon as her projection faded he would be back hunting her.

Searching, she found a single ration tube, a small water container. She burdened herself with nothing more. But at the mouth of the cave she hesitated. The night was dark and the rocks a maze. The best she could do was to find another hiding place and await Harath.

To go higher was best, reach a point from which she could see more. Thrusting the focus-stones back within her suit, Ziantha began to scramble from one hold to the next.

She was some distance from the cave when she heard a sound from below and froze, her body plastered to the cliff wall. Mauth—he was coming back! She must remain where she was lest some sound betray her.

The night was very still with no wind to howl mournfully among the erosion-sculptured stones. She could hear, sharp and clear, his movements down there, even a muttered curse which must mean he had found the cave empty. Then a second or so later came the click of the com. Was he signaling to Ogan, or receiving a message?

If she could only read that code! Dared she try mind-probe? But, even as she hesitated, Mauth was on the move again, and, by the sounds issuing from the cave, he was coming in her direction!

Then, out of the night shot a beam of dazzling light. Not to pin Ziantha to the rock, but to show Mauth.

"Freeze—right where you are!"

He obeyed and there followed sounds of others on the move—coming up. Patrolmen? They would question Mauth, learn about her. Ziantha swallowed. She was as helpless here as Mauth was, even if they had no light on her. For her slightest move would make a betraying sound.

Someone climbed into the flood of light centered on Mauth. But that was no Patrol uniform, rather a crewman's planet suit—Iuban's men then. If Yasa had made the deal Ogan expected— Should Ziantha hail them? But she could not be sure if Yasa was a free ally or Iuban's prisoner. No—stay free if she could—find Harath and learn some truths.

The crewman disarmed Mauth, was shoving him downhill. And they made no move to climb higher. They did not suspect her to be here then. But they would learn speedily enough. Ziantha had no illusion that Mauth would not tell everything they wanted to know once they applied Jack methods to the learning. As soon as she had the chance to move she should get as far away from here as possible.

They were searching the cave now. But that took no length of time. Ziantha willed them to go. She was not using the power, but sometimes even such willing could exert an influence.

Then she drew a deep breath of relief and would have sagged to the ground had there been anything more than a shallow ledge to support her. They were leaving, at last. She strained her ears to follow the sounds of their withdrawal, waiting poised for what seemed very long moments after the last of those finally died away.

Now—up and up—on! The girl began the ascent with the caution dark demanded, feeling ahead with her hands, testing each step with her foot before she put her full weight upon it. Twice she huddled, with a wildly beating heart, as dislodged stones made noises she was sure would bring the hunters straightway back to track her down.

After what seemed hours of strain, Ziantha reached the top of the rise and found it relatively smooth with no rocks to offer shelter. Which meant pushing on, across here and down the other side. Something in the air—she cringed—and then knew it for a flying thing. So this world had night life of its own. The flapping of wings sounded lazy, assured in a way that gave her courage. At least enough to start on again.

The slope on the other side seemed easier, and she was thankful for that, moving slowly, listening always for any sound. One of the stunted bushes caught at her, thorns raking out along the hand she had flung to the side to steady herself as a foot slipped.

But she lost her footing then, skidded down a slope in a loud cascade of stones and earth, bringing up against the thorny embrace of a second growth more stoutly rooted. For a moment she was too alarmed to try to move on again. Surely anyone within a good distance had heard *that!* Without thinking she tried mind-probe.

Harath!

Since she had broken their thread back in the cave she had longed to find a sanctuary from which she could again link with the alien. This was no hiding place, but from the very vigor of that pickup she knew that Harath must be near.

He must be close—very close! Seconds later she heard a faint noise—Harath on this slope?

Something was indeed moving in her direction, making less noise, Ziantha was certain, than a man. And Harath had nightsight; to him this stretch of gravel and small rocks would be much more visible than to her. She held fast to the bush as an anchor, waiting.

Scuttling—then before her—Harath!

He sprung straight for her, both pairs of his tentacles out to find holds on her body. There radiated from him a need for contact, for a meeting of body to body. Ziantha cuddled his small downy shape against her, though it seemed very odd that the usually self-sufficient Harath needed such comfort.

"You were lost?"

"Not lost! Come with Harath—come!"

His excitement was wild and now he struggled in her grasp.

"Must come—he dies!"

"Who dies?" Ogan? Had the parapsychologist met with disaster on his attempt to reach the L-B?

"He!" Harath seemed to be utterly unable to understand that Ziantha did not know. As if the person he meant was of such importance in the world that there was no question of his identity.

"Come!"

She had never seen Harath so excited before. The alien would not answer her questions, but fought for release with the same vigor as he had greeted her. That he wanted her attention for only one thing, to obey his command, was plain. And she could not control him.

He had already struggled out of her hold. Ziantha could not restrain him without applying force, and that she was not prepared to do.

"Come!" He scuttled away as swiftly as he had arrived.

Ziantha got carefully to her feet. That she must not let Harath escape her again was plain. But also she had not his sight and could not trust the path ahead.

"Harath!" Had she made that call as emphatic as she must? "Harath—you must wait—I cannot see you!"

"Come!" She caught a glimpse of movement at the foot of the slope, as if Harath lingered there, bobbing about in his impatience and desire to be gone. Recklessly she half slid, half jumped down to that level. Now he reached with an upper tentacle, took hold of her suit, tugged with all his limited strength.

"Come!"

At least Harath offered a guide. As Ziantha obeyed that tug, the girl discovered she did not have to fear such rough footing, that her companion was picking the smoothest way. There was light in the sky now, as a moon rose. A small pale moon whose radiance was of a green hue, making her own flesh look strange and unhealthy.

Harath turned east. Ziantha thought she recognized one of the oddly shaped peaks in that wan moonlight. Surely they were not far from the Jack ship.

Yasa? But Harath had insisted on "he," and the alien had never displayed any great liking for the Salarika in the past. No—she did not think he led her to the veep. Now he was showing wariness as he angled back and forth among strange outcrops of rock which arose in clusters like the petrified trunks of long dead trees.

"The Jack ship—" Ziantha ventured.

Harath did not reply; only his grasp on her suit tightened, and he gave a sharp pull as if forbidding communication here. They wound a way beyond those rocks and came to a place where pinnacles were joined at the foot to form a wall. Harath loosed his hold on her, scrambled at a speed wherein his feet were aided by all four tentacles, climbing the curve of that wall at a space between two spires.

"Come!"

Where Harath might go she was not sure she could follow. The space between those prongs of stone looked very narrow. But Ziantha had to try it or lose him entirely. Dragging herself up, she wedged between the outcrops, an action which nearly scraped the suit from her back.

Below was a depression like the one in which Ogan had earlier camped. And that pocket was full of shadow. But she could make out dimly that someone lay on the ground here, and Harath was beside the body.

Harath—and a stranger—the sensitive! But if Harath wanted her—then that other was not dead after all! Ziantha's heart beat so fast that it seemed to shake her. She went on her knees beside the body she could not see.

Now she explored with her hands. He wore the bulk of a planet suit, the heavy boots of an explorer. But his head was uncovered and he lay face up. His skin was very cold, but when she held her hand palm down over his lips she could feel a breath puff against her skin. Entranced? It might well be. If so, to bring him out would be a matter requiring more skill than she possessed. Ogan should be here.

"No—Ogan kill!"

Harath's thought was like a blow, sharp enough to make her start back.

"You—Harath—reach—reach—" The alien's communication was in her mind. The emotion of fear which her suggestion of Ogan had raised in him had upset him to the point where he could not mind-send coherently. What lay behind

188

that fear, Ziantha could not guess, but its reality she did not doubt in the least. If Harath said Ogan was a danger, she was willing to accept his verdict.

"Harath—" she sent the thought in as calm a fashion as she could summon. "How do we reach—?"

He appeared able now to control himself.

"Send—with Harath—send—"

Did he mean reverse the process that one generally used with Harath—lend her energy to the alien, rather than draw upon his as she had in the past?

"Yes, yes!" He was eager in affirmation of that.

"I will send," she agreed without further question.

With one hand she unsealed her suit, brought out the focus-stones. Whether those might lend any force to this quest she could not tell, but that they needed all the energy they could call upon now she firmly believed.

Then she leaned forward again over the limp body, touched her fingers to the cold forehead. Around her wrist closed, in a grip as tight as a punishing bond, one of Harath's tentacles. They were now linked physically as they must be linked mentally if this was to succeed.

There was a dizzy sensation of great speed, as if she—or that part of Ziantha that was her innermost self—was being swung out and out and out into a place where all was chaos and there was no stability except that tie with Harath. Farther and farther they quested. The focus-stones grew warm in her hand; she was aware of those and that from them was flowing now a steady push of energy. It passed through her body, down her arm, to those fingers, to the tentacle, where their three bodies met in touch.

Swing, swing, out and out and out—until Ziantha wanted to cry Enough! That if they ventured farther their tie with reality would snap and they would be as lost as he whom they sought and could not find.

16

The flaw in the pattern was that she could not build up any mind picture on which to focus the energy. Turan could have been such a goal, but this man she crouched over now she had never seen, could not picture as his head lay in the shadows and she had only touch to guide her. One must have such a focus—

Did Harath see humans as they were? Could he build such a mind picture as it should be built in order to search? Ziantha doubted it. For their swing was failing now, falling back in waning sweeps.

"Hunt!" Harath's urging was sharp.

"We must have a picture." She forced upon him in return her own conclusion for the reason of their failure. "Build a picture, Harath!"

Only what wavered then into her mind was so distorted that she nearly broke contact, so shocked was she by that weird figure Harath projected, a mixture, unbelievable, of his own species and Ziantha's, something which manifestly did not exist.

"We must have a true picture." They were back in the hollow, still united by touch, but warring in mind.

The alien's frustration was fast turning to rage, perhaps aimed at her because of his own inadequacies. Ziantha summoned patience.

"This is a man of my kind," she told Harath. "But if it is he who followed me into that other time, I do not know him as himself. I cannot build the picture that we need. I must see him as he really is—"

Because Harath was so aroused by their failure, which he appeared to blame on her, she feared he would withdraw altogether. Their mind-touch was snapped by his will, and his tentacle dropped from her wrist.

The moon's greenish light was on the lip of the hollow in which they crouched. If she could somehow pull the inert man at her feet up into that—

It seemed to her that there was no other way to learn what she must. Putting the Eyes into safekeeping once more, she caught the man's body, labored to pull it up to the light. But it was a struggle even though he was smaller, lighter than Ogan or one of the crewmen. Finally she brought him to where the moon touched his face.

It was hard to judge in the weird green glow, but she thought his skin as dark as that of a veteran crewman. His hair was cropped close, also, as if to make the wearing of a helmet comfortable, and it was very tightly curled against his skull.

His features were regular; he might be termed pleasantly endowed according to the standards of her kind. But what she was to do now was to learn that face, learn every portion of it as well as if she had seen it each and every day of her existence, fix it so straight in her mind that she could never forget or lose it.

Ziantha stretched out her hand, drawing fingers, with the lightest touch, across his forehead, down the bridge of his nose, tracing the generous curve of his full lips, the firm angle of his chin and jaw. So was he made and she must remember.

Harath crowded in beside her.

"Hurry—he is lost. If he is too long lost—"

She knew that ancient, eating horror of all sensitives when they evoked the trance state—to be lost out of body. But she had to make sure that she would know now whom they sought in those ways which were unlike any world her kind walked.

"I know—" Ziantha only trusted that it was now true that she did indeed know.

Once more she took the Eyes from concealment, gripped them tightly in her left hand, set the fingers of the right to the forehead of the stranger, felt Harath loop tentacle touch to her wrist.

"Now—" This time she gave the signal. But she was not aware of that swing out into the void as she had been when the alien had guided their searching. Rather she fastened in her mind, behind her closed eyes, only one thing: the stranger's face.

They were not going in search now; they were calling with all the power they possessed, all that could be summoned through the Eyes. Though she did not have a name to call upon, which would have given her efforts greater accuracy, she must use this picture to the full.

He who has this seeming—wherever he now wanders—let him—COME!

Her body, her mind became one summoning cry. That she could long hold it to this pitch she doubted. But as long as she might, that she would.

"Come!"

A stirring—faint—far away—as if something crawled painfully.

"Come!"

There was indeed an answer, weak, but aiming for her with dogged determination. She dared feel no elation, allow any thought of success to trouble the resolute pull of her call.

"Come!"

So painfully slow. And she was weakening even with the energy that flowed into her from the stones, from Harath—

"Come!"

One last effort to put into that drawing all that she had.

Then Ziantha broke, unable any longer to sustain the contact.

The girl fell face down, one arm across the body of the stranger. She was conscious, but strength was so drained out of her, she felt so weak and sick, that she could neither move nor utter a sound, even when she felt the other stir.

He pulled free of her, struggling to sit up. Harath was hopping about them both, uttering those clicks of beak that in him signaled unusual emotion. Faintly Ziantha heard the stranger mutter in some tongue that was not Basic. But there was a roaring in her own ears, a need to just lie there, unable to so much as raise a hand as the great weakness that followed her effort held her fast.

She thought the stranger was dazed, that he did not realize at first where he was or what had happened. But if that were so he made a quick recovery. For he suddenly stooped to look at her, exclaiming in his own language.

Then he lifted her up, straightening her body so she could lie in a more comfortable position, as if he well understood the malaise that gripped her. But he did not try mind-touch, for which she was grateful. Perhaps his long ordeal had exhausted his psychic energy for the time as much as the search had hers.

She watched him stand. Much of his body was still in the shadow, and what she could see gave her the impression that he was indeed short in stature and slender. But he was no boy, however much his face had given the impression of youth. That clicking blob, Harath, ran to him, scrambled up the stranger who might be now a tree to be climbed, and settled on his shoulder as if this was a perch he had known many times before.

The burden of the alien, who was no light weight, might be nothing, as the stranger pulled up between two of the rocks guarding this depression, his attitude one of listening.

Ziantha watched him. By rights she should have a long rest now—

But at last her eyes were truly focusing on the other as he turned around. He was holding night-vision glasses to his eyes, and his clothing was plain to distinguish even in this baneful moonlight. There was no mistaking the emblem on the breast of his planet suit. Patrol!

What had Harath done to her? Even Ogan—or Iuban—would have been more her friend! What could she do now? If the sensitive was Patrol, as his uniform clearly testified, he was a deadly enemy, and one who already knew from his own participation just what she was doing on this planet. There was no escape, no form of defense she could offer.

But to be erased—

Black horror worse than any fear she had ever known in her life closed about Ziantha. Harath had done this to her! She must escape—she must!

She willed her weak body to obey orders. Though she wavered to a sitting position, the girl realized that she could not escape without some aid. Harath? She could never trust him again.

Ogan. Much as she feared and now hated the parapsychologist, he did not represent the dreaded fate this stranger threatened. But if she tried to contact Ogan, with her power so depleted, either Harath, the stranger, or both, could pick up her mind-send with ease.

With her eyes, wide with fear, on the stranger, she tried to edge away, put as much space between them as possible. If she could reach the other side of this hollow, somehow crawl up—get out among the rocks— But physical efforts were useless; she did not doubt that Harath would easily track her down. The alien knew her mind-pattern and could follow it as some tracking animal might follow footprints or scent.

Yet Harath was in turn physically limited. And if she could somehow dispose of the stranger, then she might be able to out-travel the alien. Inch by inch she won away from the spot where the stranger had left her, working crabwise over the rough ground without rising to her feet. The effort it cost her left her trembling with weakness, but her will and the danger hanging over her drove her on.

She kept her attention fixed upon the other, alert to any change that would suggest he planned to join her. But he seemed intent on watching beyond the hollow, centering on it with his back half toward her. It was apparent, she believed, that he expected no trouble from her. And at that Ziantha longed to hiss as Yasa might have done.

Harath she had to fear as well, but the alien's head was also turned in the same direction as the attention of the watcher. Perhaps he was mind-searching, feeding any information he could pick up to the stranger.

In her progress Ziantha's hand closed upon a rock. With that she could perhaps bring the Patrolman down. But she greatly doubted her accuracy of aim, and to miss would alert him. Now, she could, she would, fight with all her strength if he tried to master her physically, but she must concentrate on escape. She had almost reached the point where she believed she could hope to pull up to the rim.

Only she was not going to have the chance. For the stranger in a swift movement dropped the glasses to hang on their strap and turned to slide down into the hollow. He stopped short when he saw Ziantha, not where he had left her, but with her back against the wall, the stone gripped tight as a pitiful weapon.

"What—?" he spoke Basic now.

She raised the stone. As far as she could see he wore no weapon. And certainly he must be worn from his ordeal in the limbo between Turan's world and this.

"Stand off!" she warned him.

"Why?"

Ziantha could not see him face to face, for he was again

in the shadow. But his bulk she could make out. She wondered at the surprise in his voice. Surely he knew that, being what she was, they were deadly enemies?

"Keep off," she repeated.

But he was moving toward her. If she had only left him lost! Fool to trust Harath—the alien was one with Yasa, Ogan and all the others who used her with no thought of her life.

"I mean you no harm." He stood still. "Why do you—"

She laughed then. Only it did not sound like laughter but a crazed, harsh sound that hurt as she uttered it.

"No harm? No, no more harm than a pleasant visit to the Coordinator—then to be erased!"

"No!"

He need not deny that so emphatically. Did he think she was so brain-weakened by what she had been through (and for him!) that she did not remember what happened to sensitives who served the Guild when the Patrol caught them?

"No—you do not understand—"

Weakly, but with all the strength she had, Ziantha threw the stone she held. Let him come any closer and she was lost. This was her one chance. And in the same instant as the stone left her fingers there was a burst of pain in her head, so terrible, so overwhelming, that she did not even have a chance to voice the scream it brought to her lips as she wilted down under that thrust of agony.

The storm was upon them—she must be in the tower. The Lurla—they lay curled, they would not obey, though she sent the commands. They must! If they did not, she would be thrown to the pounding waves below, and the Eyes given to one who could use them. But when she tried the Eyes were dull—they cracked and shivered into splinters, then to dust, sifting through her fingers. And she was left without any weapon.

They were high in the hills, and below them the enemy forces had gathered. But above and behind, coming steadily with fire beams to hunt them out, were flyers. This was a trap from which there was no escape. She must contrive to have death find her quickly when the jaws of the trap closed. For to be captive in the hands of those from Singakok was a worse ending than the clean death in battle. She was Vintra of the Rebels and would not live to be mocked in the streets of the city. Never! The flyers were very close, already their beams fused the hidden guns. This was death, and she must welcome it.

Heat, light, life—she was alive. And they would find her. She would be captive in Singakok— No! Let her but get her hands on her own weapons and she would make sure of that. But she could not move. Had she been wounded? So hurt in the assault that her body would not obey her?

Fearfully she opened her eyes. There was open sky above her. Of course, she lay among the Cliffs of Quait. But the sounds of the flyers were gone. It was very quiet, too quiet. Was she alone in a camp of the dead? Those dead whom she would speedily join if she could?

Sound now—someone was coming—if one of the rebels she would appeal for the mercy thrust, know it would be accorded her as was her right. She was Vintra; all men knew that she must not fall alive into the hands of the enemy—

Vintra—but there was someone else—D'Eyree! And then— Ziantha! As if thinking that name steadied a world that seemed to spin around her, she ordered her thoughts. Ziantha —that was right! Unless the Eyes had betrayed her a second time into another return. She was Ziantha and Ziantha was—

Her memory seemed oddly full of holes as if parts of it had been extracted to frighten her. Then she looked up at a down-furred body perched on two legs ending in clawed feet, a body leaning over her so round eyes could stare directly into hers.

This was Ziantha's memory. And that was—Harath! At first she was joyfully surprised. Then memory was whole. Harath was an enemy. She fought to move, to even raise her hand—uselessly. But on wriggling hard to gaze along her body she saw the telltale cords of a tangler. She was a prisoner, and she could share to the full Vintra's despair and hatred for those who had taken her.

That Harath had changed sides did not surprise her now. He was an alien, and as such he was not to be subjected to erasure or any of the penalties the Patrol would inflict on her. Undoubtedly he would aid them as he had Ogan in the past.

Ziantha made no effort to use mind-touch. Why should she? Harath had seemed so much in accord with the stranger she did not believe she could win him back. He had been too frantic when he had begged her aid to redeem the other's lost personality. What a fool she had been to answer his call!

She no longer wanted to look at Harath, wedged her head around so she could see only sunlit rock. This was not the same hollow in which she had been struck down. They were in a more open space. And now she could view the stranger also.

He lay some distance away, belly down, on what might be the edge of a drop, his head at an angle to watch below. Then she heard the crackle of weapon fire. Somewhere on a lower level a struggle was in progress.

Ziantha heard the sharp click of Harath's bill, apparently he was trying to gain her attention. Stubbornly she kept her eyes turned from him, her mind-barrier up. Harath had betrayed her; she wanted no more contact with him. There came a sharp and painful pull of her hair. By force her head was dragged around, Harath had her in tentacle grip. And, though she closed her eyes instantly against his compelling gaze, Ziantha could feel the force of his mind-probe seeking to reach her. There was no use wasting power she might need later in such a small struggle. She allowed mind-touch.

"Why do you fear?"

She could not believe that Harath would ask that. Surely he well knew what they would do to her.

"You—you gave me to the Patrol. They will—kill my talent, that which is me!" she hurled back.

"Not so! This one, he seeks to understand. Without him you might be dead."

She thought of her escape from D'Eyree's tomb. Better she had died there. What would come out of erasure would no longer be Ziantha!

"Better I had died," she replied.

She was looking straight up into Harath's eyes. Suddenly he loosed his hold on her hair, dropped mind-touch. She watched him cross the rock, his beak clicking as if he chewed so on her words, joining the man who still lay watching the battle below.

Harath uncoiled a tentacle, reached out to touch the stranger's hand. Ziantha saw the other's head turn, though she could catch only a very foreshadowed view of his brown face. She was sure that Harath and he were in communication, but she did not try to probe for any passage of thought between them.

Then the stranger rolled over to look at her. When she stared back, hostile and defiant, he shrugged, as if this was of no matter, returning to his view below.

There was a sound. Under them the rock vibrated. Up over the cliff rose the nose of a ship, pointed outward, the flames of her rockets heating the air. On she climbed and was gone, with a roar, leaving them temporarily deaf.

Surely not Ogan's L-B. Such a craft was far too small to have made such a spectacular take-off. That must have been the Jack ship! The girl lost all hope now; she had been left in

Patrol hands. Ziantha could have wailed aloud. But pride was stubborn enough to keep her lips locked on any weakling whimper.

Who had driven the Jack ship off? The Patrol? Ogan? If the latter, he must have been reinforced. If so, feverishly her mind fastened on that, Ogan was still here—she could reach him—

The stranger walked back toward her, standing now as if he feared no danger of detection. She could see him clearly. Turan she had learned to know, even when she realized that his body was only a garment worn by another. But now more than the uniform this one wore was a barrier between them. There was not only the fear of the Patrol but a kind of shyness.

In the past, on Korwar, she had lived a most retired life. Those forays Yasa had sent her on were tasks upon which it was necessary to concentrate deeply, so that during them she observed only those things that applied directly to the failure or success of her mission. Yasa's inner household had been largely female, Ziantha's life therein strictly ordered as if she were some dedicated priestess—which in a way, she had been.

Ogan had never seemed a man, but rather a master of the craft which exercised her talents—impersonal, remote, a source of awe and sometimes of fear. And the various male underlings of the household had been servants, hardly more lifelike to her than a more efficient metal robo.

But this was a man with a talent akin to hers, equal, she believed. And she could not forget the actions on Turan's time level that had endangered them both, that they had shared as comrades, though he was now the enemy. He made her feel self-conscious, wary in a way she had not experienced before.

Yet he was not in any way imposing; only a fraction perhaps over middle height, and so slender it made him seem less. She had been right about the hue of his skin: that was a warm dark brown, which she was sure was natural, and not induced by long exposure to space. And his hair, in the sun, shone in tight black curls. Of Terran descent she was sure, but he could be a mutation, as so many of the First Wave colonists now were, tens and hundreds of generations later.

He settled down beside her, watching her thoughtfully as if she presented some type of equation he must solve. And because she found that silence between them frightening, she asked a question:

"What ship lifted then?"

"The Jacks'. They tangled with some of their own, at least it looked so. Beat the attackers off, then lifted. But there was not much left of the opposition. I think a couple, three at the most, made it out of range when the ship blasted."

"Ogan! He will be after—" she said eagerly and then could have bitten her tongue in anger at that self-betrayal.

"After you? No—he cannot trace us even if he wants to. We have a shield up no one can break."

"So what are you going to do now?" Ziantha came directly to the point, unwillingly conceding that he might be truthful. No one should underrate the Patrol.

"For a time we wait. And while we do so, this is a good time to make you understand that I do not want to hold you like this." He pointed to the tangler cords which restrained her so completely.

"Do you expect me to promise no attempts to escape, with erasure awaiting me?"

"What would you escape to? This is not exactly a welcoming world." There was a reasonableness in his words that awoke irritation in her. "Food, water—and those others"—now he waved to the cliff—"wandering around. You are far safer here. Safer than you might be in Singakok that was." For the first time he gave indication that he remembered their shared past. "At least the High Consort is not setting her hounds to our trail."

He took a packet of smoke sticks from a seal pocket, snapped the end of one alight, and inhaled thoughtfully the sweet scent. By all appearances he was as much at ease as he would be in some pleasure palace on Korwar, and his placidity fed her irritation.

"What are we waiting for?" Ziantha demanded, determined to know the worst as soon as possible.

"For a chance to get back to my ship. I do not intend to carry you all the way there. In fact, since I may have to fight for the privilege of seeing it again, I could not if I would. There is an alarm broadcast going out; the Patrol ship in this region must already have picked it up. We can expect company, and we can wait for it here. Unless you are reasonable and agree to make no trouble. Then we shall make for the scout and be, I assure you, far more comfortable."

"Comfortable for you—not for me. When I know what is before me!"

He sighed. "I wish you would listen and not believe that you already know all the answers."

"With the Patrol I do—as far as I am concerned!" she flared.

"And who said," he returned calmly, "that I represent the Patrol?"

17

For a moment Ziantha did not understand. When she did she smiled derisively. What a fool he must believe her to think she would accept that. When he sat before her wearing a Patrol uniform. When—

"Clothes," he continued, "do not necessarily denote status. Yes, I have been working with the Patrol. But on my own account, and I do this only for a space because my case seemed to match one of theirs. You see, I have been hunting the Eyes—without knowing just what I sought—for a long time."

The Eyes! Where were they now—in his keeping? Ziantha wriggled her shoulders in an abortive struggle against the cords and desisted at once when they tightened warningly about her with a pressure sharp enough to teach a lesson.

"They are still yours." He might have been reading her thoughts, though she was unaware of any probe.

"If you are not Patrol—then who are you—wearing that insignia?" She made that a challenge, refusing to believe that he was more than trying to lull her for his own purposes.

"I am a sensitive associated with the Hist-Techneer Zorb-jac, leader of a Zacathan expedition to X One. And for your information X One is the sister planet of this in the Yaka system." He inhaled from the scented stick again. Harath clawed his way up over the rocks behind, as if he had been on a scouting expedition, and settled down by the stranger's knee.

"Ogan there." The alien's thoughts were open. "One other —hurt. The rest are dead."

He snapped out his tentacles and took to smoothing his body down with the same unconcern the stranger displayed.

"A year ago," the other continued, "finds made on X One were plundered by a Jack force. I was asked to trace down the stolen objects, since my field is archaeological psychometry. I followed the trail to Korwar. We recovered seven pieces there; that is when I joined forces with the Patrol. The eighth was the Eye you apported from Jucundus's place. The backlash of that apport was what set me on your track—that and Harath." He dropped one hand to the alien's head in a caress to which Harath responded with a broadcast of content.

"Then—was it you at Waystar, too?"

"Yes. When the apport was made I was certain that a sensitive would know what it was, try to trace it. We have our people on Waystar; they alert us as to unusual finds that come in as loot. During the past seasons we have built up a loose accord with a couple of the Jack captains, offering them more than they can get from fences to sell us pieces of information."

"How did you get Harath to join you?"

He laughed. "Ask him that. He came to me on Korwar of his own. I gathered that he had not been too happy at the use Ogan made of him. And I knew that he could serve as a link with you when I might need one. I was right, as you were willing to link with him at once—though I did not bargain for that linkage to be so tight as to pull me into Turan." He grimaced. "That was a challenge I would not want to face again."

"You knew about the Eyes all the time!" She had an odd feeling of being cheated, as if she had performed a difficult task to no purpose at all.

"Not so! I knew that that ugly little lump Jucundus bought was something more powerful than it looked to be.

One could sense that easily. But the Eyes—no, I had no idea of their existence. What they are seems to be infinitely greater than any discovery the Zacathans have made in centuries."

"But," Ziantha came directly back to the part of his story that shadowed her future, "you joined with the Patrol to run us down. You wear their uniform."

He sighed. "It was necessary for me to take rank for a while. I am *not* Patrol."

"Then who are you?"

Again he laughed. "I see that I have been backward in the ordinary courtesies of life, gentle fem. My name is Ris Lantee, and I am Wyvern trained if that means anything—"

"It means," she flashed, "that you are a liar! Everyone knows that the Wyverns do not deal with males!"

"That is so," he agreed readily. "Most males. But I was born on their world; my parents are mind-linked liaison officers, both of whom the Wyvern council have accepted. When I was born with the power, they bowed to the fact I possessed it, and they gave me training. Can one sensitive lie to another?"

Though he invited her probe with that, Ziantha was reluctant to let her own barrier down. To hold it against him was her defense. He waited, and when she did not try to test his response, he frowned slightly.

"We waste time with your suspicions," he commented. "Though I suppose they are to be expected. But would I open my mind if I were trying to conceal anything from you? You know that is impossible."

"So far I have thought it impossible. But you say you are Wyvern trained, and the Wyverns deal with hallucinations—"

"You are well schooled."

"Ogan gathered information on every variation of the power known—and some only the Guild know," she answered. "I was given every warning."

205

"That, too, is to be expected."

"If you are not Patrol"—she pushed aside everything now but what was most important to her—"what do you intend to do with me? Turn me over for erasure when their ship planets in? You know the law."

"It all depends—"

"Upon what—or whom?" Ziantha continued to press.

"Mainly upon you. Give me your word you will not try to escape. Let us go back to my scout."

Ziantha tried to weigh her chances without emotion. Ogan was free; she had no reason to doubt Harath's report. He had said he had hidden a detect-safe L-B connected by a timer to a ship. Therefore he had a way of escape. The Jack ship had lifted; she could not depend on any assistance from Yasa. In fact she was sure she had already been discarded as far as the Salarika veep was concerned. Yasa was never one to hesitate cutting losses.

And somehow, between Ogan and this Ris Lantee, she inclined to trust the latter, even though he admitted connection with the Patrol. At least with freedom she might have a better chance for the future.

"As you have said," she spoke sullenly, trying to let him believe she surrendered because there was no other choice, "where could I escape to? For now, I promise."

"Fair enough." He touched the tangler cords in two places with the point of his belt knife, and they withered away.

Ziantha sat up, rubbing her wrists. Hands fell on her shoulders, drawing her to her feet, steadying her as she moved on stiff limbs.

"Do the Zacathans know about Singakok?" she asked as they went.

Harath had climbed up Lantee, was settled on his shoulder. But the man's hand was under her arm, ready with support when she needed, and they made their way down a steep slope.

206

"About Singakok—no. But there are ruins on X One that are in a fair state of preservation. Perhaps those who peopled this world—the survivors—fled there after whatever catastrophe turned Singakok into this. As Turan, I recognized a kinship between the buildings of the past and those ruins. And with the aid of the Eyes what will we not be able to discover!" There was excitement in his voice.

"You—you would be willing to evoke the past again—after what happened?" Ziantha was surprised at this. Had she been the one lost in that awful limbo that he entered when he could no longer fight off Turan's "death," she would have fled full speed from such a trip again.

"This time one could go prepared." His confidence was firmly assured. "There would be safeguards, as there are for deep trances. Yes, I would be willing to evoke the past again. Would you?"

To admit her fear was difficult. Yet he would learn it at once if she ever relaxed the barrier between them.

"I do not know."

"I think that you could not deny your own desire to learn if you were given free choice—"

He was interrupted by a wild clicking of Harath's beak. Lantee's arm swung up, formed a barrier against her advance.

"Ogan is near."

"You said you have what can safeguard us?"

"Against mental invasion, yes. Just as you hold a barrier for me now. But if Ogan has some means of stepping up power it may be that we must unite against him, the three of us. I do not underestimate this man; he cannot be taken lightly even when he is on the run."

This was her chance. But, no, the word she had given was as tangible a bond as the tangler cords had been. Nor was she sure, even if that promise did not exist, that she would have left these two, sought out Ogan.

"What can he bring against us?" Lantee continued.

"I do not know," she was forced to confess. What equipment was small enough to be packed personally Ziantha could not tell. The Guild was notorious for its gathering of unusual devices. Ogan might even have the equivalent of the Eyes.

"I—" she was beginning when the world around her blurred. The rocks, the withered-looking vegetation, rippled as if all were painted on a curtain stirred by the wind. The change was such to frighten, passing from desolation to land alive.

She stood on a street between two lines of buildings. Before her stretched the length of a city, towering against the brilliances of sunlit sky. People moved, afoot, in vehicles—yet about them was something unreal.

Ziantha gasped, tried to leap aside as a landcar bore straight for her. But she was not allowed to escape; a grasp held her firmly in spite of her cries, her struggles. Then, the car was upon her but there was no impact, nothing! Another came the other way, scraped by her. She shut her eyes against those terrors and went on fighting what held her helpless in the Singakok returned—for this was Singakok.

The Eyes—they had done this! Yet she had not focused upon them. And if they were able to do this without her willing—! She raised her free hand to her breast. Unsealing her pocket slit, she snatched forth the Eyes, hurled them from her.

But she was still in Singakok! Locked in Singakok! Ziantha screamed. With a last surge of strength, backed by panic, she beat with her free hand against that thing which held her, fighting with fist, both feet, in any way she could, to break the hold. While around her—*through* her—the people and cars of the long-dead city went their way.

"Ziantha!"

She had closed her eyes to Singakok. Now she realized that, for all the seeming reality of the city, there had been no sound. Her name called in that demand for attention was real. But she dared not open her eyes.

"Ziantha!" Hands held her in spite of her fierce struggles. And the hands were as real as the voice.

"What do you see?" The demand came clearly, to compel her answer.

"I—I stand in Singakok—" And because her fear was so great she released the barrier against mind-probe.

Instantly touch flowed in, that same strong sense of comradeship she had known with Turan. She no longer fought, but rather stood trembling, allowing the confidence he radiated to still her panic, bring stability. And—she had been a fool not to allow this before—he did not mean her ill! As they had fought together in Singakok, as he had given of his last strength to aid her out of Nornoch, so was he prepared to stand with her now.

Ziantha opened her eyes. The city was still there; it made her giddy to see the cars, the pedestrians, and know that this was hallucination. But who induced it? Not the Wyvern-trained Lantee—he could not have done so and responded to her mental contact as he was now doing. Harath? The Eyes? But those she had thrown away.

"The Eyes! I threw them away, but still I see Singakok!" She quavered.

"You see a memory someone is replaying for you. Ogan—" Lantee's voice from close beside her, even as she could hold on to him. But she could not *see* him—only Singakok.

"Do not look, use your mind sense," Lantee ordered. "Do you pick up any thoughts?"

She tested. There was Lantee—Harath—nothing of those alien patterns she had known before. Just as the city had no sounds to make it real to one sense, so it had no mind-pattern to make it real to another.

"It is sight—my sight—"

"Well enough." Lantee's voice was as even as if he fully

understood what was happening. "The hallucination is only for one sense. It worked in that it made you throw away the Eyes."

Sent to force her to discard the Eyes? Then it had succeeded.

"I did. I threw them—"

"Not very far. And Harath has retrieved them. Now listen, this was meant to engulf us all. But because I am Wyvern trained, and because Harath is alien, we were not caught. But if we stay here to fight for your freedom we may be courting another and stronger attack. Therefore we must push on. You must discount what you see, depend upon mind-send and your other senses, so we can reach my scout. Do you understand?"

"Yes." Ziantha kept her eyes tightly closed. Could she walk so blind, even with them leading her?

"We can do it." Lantee was confident. "Keep your eyes closed if you must, but follow our directions. Harath will work directly with you. I am now putting him on your shoulder."

She felt the weight, the painfully strong clutch of Harath's claws.

"Keep your eyes closed. Harath wishes to try something."

She felt the touch of the alien's tentacles about her head; then their tips were lightly touched to her eyelids. It—it was like seeing and yet unlike—the sensation was strange. But through Harath she could visualize the scene as it had been before the illusion entrapped her. And, with her hand in Lantee's, as he drew her on, with Harath's shared sight, Ziantha started ahead. She went with only a shaky belief that this could be done, but her confidence grew.

They were following one of the small stream trickles now, and, remembering the poisonous lizard, she projected a warning. Lantee reassured her.

"We are sending warn-off vibrations. You need not worry about the native life."

"This is the long way round," he added a moment later. "Ogan may have more weapons. We have the shield; but since he has been able to pierce that in your case, we cannot be sure he will not try more direct methods of attack."

More direct methods of attack—laser fire from ambush? No, she must not let herself think of that, she must concentrate on the journey. There were differences in Harath's sight and her own as she speedily discovered, a distortion that was a trial. But it was far better than being led blindly.

They toiled up a rise where Ziantha found the going harder than it had been before. And there was a second descent as both Harath and Lantee cautioned her, taking so long on the passage down, she felt they would never reach bottom.

But before them stood a ship. Far smaller than the Jack craft that had once been a trader, this, she presumed—though through Harath's intermediacy its outlines were odd—was the Patrol scout.

"Wait!" Lantee's hand was now an anchor.

"What is the matter?" Through Harath Ziantha could not see anything that might be amiss. But this perception could be deceptive.

"The ship—it was left on persona-lock—with the ramp in!"

"But the ramp"—with Harath's aid she could see that—"it is out!"

"Just so. Walk into a trap. Does he think he has panicked us into being utter fools? If so he is wrong—but—"

Ziantha stiffened. "Is it not the ship. He *wants* you to try for that—"

She could hear his heightened breathing, so still he was. Harath had tensed in turn on her shoulder until his claws cut her flesh. She welcomed that pain as a tie with reality.

"A distort! Can you not feel it?" Surely he was aware of

that stomach turning, that inner churning, as if mind and body were swinging about.

It was growing so much stronger that she knew she could force herself no nearer. Now she felt Harath's tentacles slip from their hold about her head, their touch gone from her eyelids. She no longer had his sense as her guide, while that terrible feeling of disorientation grew and grew.

Harath uttered a shrill cry, carrying the force of a human scream. Apparently he was more susceptible to this attack than even the other two. He lost his hold, and Ziantha caught him, felt the shudders in his body. As she cradled him against her he went limp and she lost his mind-touch.

"Back!" Lantee drew her with him. But the distort centered on them, followed their retreat. Whatever defensive barrier her companion trusted in had not held. And if they were caught by the full force of a powerful distort they could lose all coherent thought.

"I am stepping up barrier power." Lantee's voice had not changed; he still seemed confident. "But," he continued, "that cannot hold too long."

"And when it blows—" she added what he had not said, "we can be overcome."

"There is one thing—"

He pulled at her hand. "Get down, behind these rocks." Gently he forced her to her knees. The distort broadcast lessened.

"You say there is something we can do?"

"You have the Eyes."

"I threw them away back there. Harath—"

"Harath returned them to me. Here." His hands on hers, opening her fist, dropping on her flattened palm those two pieces of mineral.

"Since you have used them, they will answer best to you. Now, Ogan has plunged you into a visual hallucination. He is hiding near here somewhere. He could not have forced

212

entrance to the ship, although he hallucinates for us that he has. We must reverse on him his own illusion."

"Can this be done?" She had heard of the master illusionists of Warlock, these Wyverns who ruled with dreams and could make anyone falling under their influence live in a world they had created. Lantee was Wyvern trained, but she had never heard of engulfing someone in his own hallucination.

"We cannot tell until we try. Singakok is your illusion. If we can—we shall send him to Singakok!"

Ziantha gasped. She had never heard of such trial of power. But then she *had* heard strange things of what the Wyverns could do with their dream control. And—she was suddenly sure of one thing—that Lantee could be depended upon in a way she had never dared to depend upon anyone in the past. Yasa, Ogan, for them she was a tool. Lantee sought to use her talent now, but as a part of a combined action from which they might both benefit.

"I—I have never tried this." She moistened her lips, unwilling to let him think that she was more able than she was.

"I have—a little. But this is a full test. Now—open your eyes. Look upon Singakok, if we are still within its boundaries. If not, look upon the land about, focus on it through the stones. Make it as real as you can."

She was afraid, afraid of the city, of what might happen when she did focus, afraid of being once more drawn back into the past. Resolutely she made herself face that fear, acknowledge it, and set it aside.

Pressing the Eyes against her forehead as D'Eyree had to release their maximum energy, Ziantha opened her eyes. She was not on a city street this time, rather in a garden, and before her was the rise of a building that was not unlike the palace of the Lord Commander, though she was sure this was not the same. There were guards at the door; men came and went, as if this were a place in which important affairs were conducted. Since she had not Vintra's memories now she could not identify this place. But it was so real except for the silence that she could hardly believe she had not been plunged once more into the past.

"Hold!" At this order she concentrated with all the power she could summon on the scene, trying, where any detail was hazy, to build more solidly.

What Lantee was doing, she could not guess. And Harath was still a limp weight on her arm. But she held the scene with a fierce intensity. Though it was getting harder to keep those details in such clear relief.

There was a sudden fluttering of the whole landscape before her. It became a painted curtain, torn across, and through those rents Ziantha could see rocks and beyond them the ship standing like a finger pointing to the freedom of space.

Then—the illusion was gone!

At the same time that sick feeling, born of the distort, also vanished. She was free! Ziantha scrambled to her feet, Harath stirring against her. Crouched still on his knees, his face in his hands, was Lantee. When he did not move she took a step forward, placed the hand still holding the Eyes on his shoulder.

He quivered under her touch, raised his head. His eyes were shut, his skin beaded with moisture.

"Ris?" She made a question of his name.

He opened his eyes. At first she feared he was caught in just such an illusion as the one which had held her for so long. Then he blinked and knew her. But before she could speak there came a cry from beyond. As one they turned to look.

From between two mounds of earth staggered Ogan, his hands to his head. He uttered sharp, senseless cries as he ran, making curious detours as if he swerved to avoid things which were not there.

"Come." Lantee held out his hand.

She held back. "He'll see us—"

"He sees Singakok. But how long that will continue I do not know. We must go before the illusion breaks."

Ogan, still crying out, was running along beside the rocks behind which they had taken refuge. Hand in hand they sprinted for the ship, passing him, but he did not heed them. Lantee had a com to his lips; he uttered into it the code to open the hatch, really extend the ramp.

Panting, Ziantha drew herself up that boarding way as fast as she could, Lantee serving as a rear guard. She expected at any moment to be struck again by the distort wave, yet she reached the hatch and that attack did not come.

"Up!" The interior was cramped in comparison with the two ships she had known. She climbed the ladder in the same breathless haste as she had taken the ramp. Behind Lantee the hatch clanged shut.

The control cabin at last and Lantee pushed her into one of the webbing seats, pressed the button to weave the take-off binding over her and Harath together. He was in the pilot's place, his fingers busy with the controls.

She felt the shock of lift-off and blacked out.

A trickle of moisture down her chin. Lantee bent over her, forcing the spout of a revi-tube into her mouth. As that instant energy flowed into her, Ziantha straightened within the webbing.

"Where—?"

"Where are we going? To X One."

"And Ogan?"

"Can wait for the Patrol."

"He will talk." She was sure of that. Perhaps Lantee had given her a breathing space, but he could not stand against the Patrol. Sooner or later they would be after her.

She had forgotten her mind-barrier was down; now she saw him shake his head.

"If they come—that is not going to do them any good. The Zacathans do not often take a hand in human affairs, but when they do, it is to some purpose."

"Why would they protect me?"

"Because, Ziantha-Vintra-D'Eyree, you are about the most important find, as far as they are concerned, of this age. You opened a new doorway, and they are going to bend every effort to keep it open. Do you suppose they would let your gift be erased?"

He seemed so sure; he believed in what he said. She wished she could, too.

Again he knew her thoughts.

"Just try to—try to believe one impossible thing a day, and you will find it the truth. What you did down there"—Lantee waved to the visa-screen, where the world of Singakok was fast growing smaller—"was impossible, was it not? You died twice, I died once, but can you deny we are alive? Knowing that, why can you not think that the future is brighter than you fear?"

"I guess because it never has been," Ziantha answered slowly. But he was right. Death was said to be the end, but twice she had passed that end. So—she drew a deep breath. Maybe this was all illusion, like the one they had left Ogan trapped in. If so—let it hold.

Lantee was smiling, and in her arms Harath gave a soft click of beak.

"You will see—it shall!" Somehow both their thoughts came at once with bright promise to warm her mind, just as the Eyes waited warmly in her hand. Waiting for the next illusion—the next adventure?